The S(

Tecumseh's Gold

Jeff Darnell

BookLocker
Saint Petersburg, Florida

Print ISBN: 978-1-64718-752-1
Epub ISBN: 978-1-64718-753-8
Mobi ISBN: 978-1-64718-754-5

Published by BookLocker.com, Inc., St. Petersburg, Florida.

Printed on acid-free paper.

BookLocker.com, Inc.
2020

First Edition

Library of Congress Cataloging in Publication Data
Darnell, Jeff
The Secret of Tecumseh's Gold by Jeff Darnell
Library of Congress Control Number: 2020913570

This book is dedicated to my lovely wife, Christene, and our wonderful children, Shelby and Zach.

Acknowledgments

I would like to express gratitude to my dear friends Kelly Townsend, Vint Moore and Dave Murphy for their constructive input after a proofread of my first draft. My thanks also go to the White County Historical Society, and staff, as well as the Monticello-Union Township Public Library, and their staff. Everyone was very gracious with their time and assistance. Last but not least, my thanks go to editor David Aretha for his marvelous work. You can learn more about David by visiting his website, www.davidaretha.com.

Author's Note

This book was a lot of fun for me to write. It is a sequel to a prior book, *The Mystery of the Tomahawk Pipe*. I knew there was more to write about. I liked the characters, and I liked the historical fiction story built around the legend of Tecumseh's hidden gold.

The legend is a fact. The Prologue in my prior book was a verbatim newspaper article printed in the *Cincinnati Post* on January 25, 2000. That article was not manufactured by me. It planted the seed in my head to build some fictional characters around the legend.

Because this book is a sequel, it requires what I believe to be a tedious recap of the original story for the benefit of those who did not read the first book. That recap is in Chapter 2. Thank you in advance for wading through it.

I admit to creative license with some of the material in this book. The necessity was due to my lack of not being able to do onsite research because of the COVID-19 pandemic during the time of my writing. One of these items involved the building of the Oakdale Dam south of Monticello, Indiana. I had to assume the construction involved building a temporary channel around the dam for the river, which was subsequently filled upon completion of the project. Many dams are built this way. I would have liked to have confirmed it by visiting Monticello to research records but could not do so. Likewise, I would have also researched the names of the stores and buildings present around the courthouse square in 1925 to provide a more accurate description.

I hope you enjoy the story.

Chapter 1

White County, Indiana, July 1854

The old man dipped his paddle into the creek and pushed his dugout farther upstream. Strange, he thought, how many times he had made this same journey over his lifetime. This, though, would be the last. There would be no need to come to this spot, again, after today. Besides, Nipoowi would surely come to him before many more moons and his spirit would then join those in the afterlife.

Fog lifted as the morning sun burned it off, the scent of honeysuckle and Queen Anne's lace lifting with it. Frogs leapt off the banks as the canoe passed. The old man closed his eyes and drifted. A breeze rustled the leaves of the sycamores and cottonwoods that lined both sides of the creek. The sounds and smells of the early morning always made him think back to his childhood.

He had been born into a Mekoche tribe of the Wapakoneta Shawnee, and the raucous infant was given the name Abooksigun, the wildcat. As a boy he completed his pa-wa-kah, his trials to manhood, and it was then the mighty Black Hoof took him to meet a young chieftain, Tecumseh, with whom he forged a fastness and respect that remained these many years later.

He grew into a young brave, followed Tecumseh and his growing band into skirmishes against the wasicu, the white devils, then followed the chieftain out of Ohio into the Indiana Territory. With his brother, The Prophet, Tecumseh established a new settlement on the bluffs of the Wabash River to which thousands flocked. Here they would be pushed no more. Warriors from the Miami, Iroquois, Chickamauga, Ojibway, Mascouten, Kickapoos, Winnebagos, Wyandot, Piankashaw, Seneca, Wea, Fox, Sac, and Potawatomi nations joined the Shawnee at Prophetstown to fight the ever-encroaching whites.

In 1811, the warriors needed guns. Tecumseh secretly gathered sixteen of his most trusted warriors and instructed them to journey to Canada with two hundred bars of gold to buy guns from the British. Abooksigun was among them. Each warrior made a vow to Manitou, the Great Spirit: The gold would be used for no other reason; it must be used to fight the white devils and recapture what had been taken from them. But, short into their journey, the warriors happened upon white militia, and to keep the gold from falling into hands of the whites, they hid it in a cave along a creek. Half of the warriors were killed in the battle. Those who were not each made a second vow: They would never tell others where the gold was hidden, and they would watch over it to make sure no others discovered and removed it.

Upon their return to Prophetstown they learned Tecumseh had left to recruit more warriors among the northern tribes. Shortly thereafter, Prophetstown was attacked by American forces under William Henry Harrison. The warriors were defeated, and the settlement was burned to the ground along with their fields of corn. Abooksigun and the surviving warriors followed Tecumseh north to fight the Americans alongside the British, but when Tecumseh was killed at the Battle of the Thames in Ontario, Canada, the dreams of the Indian confederation died with him.

Abooksigun and the last few braves from Tecumseh's original secret pact returned to the Indiana Territory. They had to keep their vow to watch over the gold—they must wait for another great chief to rise up and lead the people against the whites. Seasons passed. Years passed. All but Abooksigun had died. He was alone. Even his own son, Askuwheteau, had left him—angered that his father would not trust him with the secret.

Once, when the fever was bad, and he was certain Nipoowi was upon him, he had sought help from a young white frontier doctor who had built a cabin on the banks of the creek. With help from the doctor, the sickness passed. But, Abooksigun realized he had to plan for the future. He would die sometime, and he could not let the secret of the gold die with him. He had to pass it to another as a safeguard. With no one else he could trust, and knowing the young white to be honorable, Abooksigun gave him the secret of the gold's location even though the young white was unaware he was doing so at the time. Abooksigun gave the young doctor the gift of a tomahawk pipe—a beautifully carved and painted ritual pipe. It was a trick taught him many years ago by Tecumseh. A message could be coded into the carvings that only one of The People could decipher. To the unknowing, it would appear to be an ornate pipe, nothing more. In doing so, the secret could be passed and preserved. It might eventually find its way to one of The People.

Thus, to the young doctor, the pipe was simply a gift from Abooksigun for nursing him back to health. Throughout his life he had in his possession the location of a treasure and never knew it.

The gold was safe for many years, but now countless more whites had settled on farms, and a railroad was being built not far from the creek. The gold must be moved, or Abooksigun must chance its discovery by others.

Abooksigun opened his eyes and again dipped his paddle into the creek. He was in no hurry. Old men cannot be. He lifted his weathered face and squinted at the sun through the lifting fog. He had time to make one more trip before the white workers began their day. He saw in front of him a sharp bend in the creek. He was almost there.

Rounding the bend, he came to a solid rock wall with a fissure just large enough for a small man to squeeze through. He took a grass rope and with both hands wedged the rope into a small crack in the rock face. He tied the other end to the dugout so it would not float away. He carefully lowered one leg into the creek, felt for the bottom, and lifted the rest of his body out of the canoe. He'd had to wait until the dry season, when the water was low enough to allow him to stand in the creek. Even so, it was still chest high and the current was tricky.

He worked his way along the rock wall to the fissure, turned sideways, and carefully worked his way through. Once inside the small cave he waited a moment until his eyes adjusted to the dim light. The chamber was about eight feet deep and five feet wide. He had to stoop a little to not hit his head on the roof of the cave. He took a deep breath and lowered himself into the water, felt with his hands, and pulled up a smooth stone bar. Even in the shadows of the cave, the reflections of light off the water showed the luster of the gold. Abooksigun was always taken by the weight of the dense metal. Funny that a thing so small required such strength to handle it.

He slowly inched his way to the opening and out into the creek. He placed the gold bar on the floor of the dugout, then made his way back for another, and another, and another, placing each for good balance.

With the seventh stone in the canoe, he paused. It was the last of the gold bars—no more remained in the cave. How many times had he made this same trip to move all the others? It had started with the last new moon. And, now, there would be another new moon tonight. He had made many trips. But this was the last, and it troubled him. If the time should come when the yellow metal was needed, how would any of The People know where to look? The vows—even the message on the pipe given to the white doctor—pointed to this place. He must leave a message for others to find, should they look. The old man stood waist deep in the creek, hands holding onto the dugout with a bowed head. Slowly he looked up, nodded his head, grinned, and thought, yes, it is a good plan.

He slowly worked his way back into the dugout and turned over the last bar of yellow metal so that the flat bottom of it faced him. He drew his knife from its deerskin sheaf and etched into the flat surface of the yellow bar.

Once more he slid out of the dugout and into the water. He reached back into the dugout, grabbed the yellow bar and carried it back toward the opening of the little cave, slowly working his way through the current of the creek. He turned sideways, squeezed through, and moved to the center of the small cave. He looked to make sure the golden bar was sitting in his hands properly—the flat bottom with his etching down. He took a breath and then lowered it to the sandy bottom and firmly pushed it into its resting place. Rising, he paused. Yes, it is good. *My work is almost done.*

He paddled his dugout down the creek and looked at all the familiar sights—a boulder jutting up from the water here, a large sycamore hanging over the bank there. *I may never see these again. This is my last time. No need to make the journey to this place again.* He was not sad—it was simply the truth.

The dugout reached the mouth of the creek and the old man worked his way out into the larger river and turned south, staying close to the east bank. He let the current carry the dugout, using his paddle as a steering tiller. He passed under the new bridge that carried the railroad and looked to the opposite bank. He could see and hear people in the town starting their day. He always shied away from contact with them and only went to the town when he had to trade for sugar, flour, and coffee.

Mile after mile the river wound like a snake. He let the current take him. The sun was directly above in the sky now. It would not be long. He was almost there. He saw the familiar point of the sandbar jutting into the river and worked the dugout around the sharp bend, then back up into a small horseshoe-shaped hollow that cut back into the land. The little cove was perfectly protected from the flow of the river. He let the weight of the dugout slide up onto the sandy beach and then allowed himself to sit and rest. He thought about the years from long ago, of Tecumseh and the original band of warriors who had been charged with this secret. *Yes, my brothers. I have kept our vows, but I am almost finished.*

He picked up the first of the bars from the bottom of the dugout, cradled it with his two arms, stepped out of the dugout, and slowly walked up the sandy path he'd forged through the underbrush, vines, and trees. A rock cliff formed part of the face of the bluff. Abooksigun walked straight to it. Only standing close in front of the wall could he see the shallow indentation— a shallow, natural alcove in the face of the cliff. From afar it blended in with the rest of the rocky face.

He stepped into the alcove and could then see the low opening of the cave on the right, close to the ground. This was the hardest part. On hands and knees he reached out and placed the yellow bar on the ground in front of him, crawled to it, moved it farther in front of him, crawled to it, and continued the process as he moved into the darkness of the cave.

Once inside, the space opened and he could stand. He paused for a moment and let his eyes adjust. He looked to the far end of the cave, and even in the poor light the wall of golden bars reflected a yellow glow. Yes, he thought. They are wondrous to look at. He placed the new bar on the pile, sat down to rest on the cool sandy floor, and leaned back against the yellow metal to rest before the repeated trips to fetch the others from the canoe.

A few hours later, he had finally made the last trip to the cave. The task was done, now all of the gold had been safely moved to a new place, miles away from the ever-growing town. *There will be no whites working here. No farmers, no railroads. There is no need for any of them to come to this place, to the bottom of this cliff below the bluff.*

Scattered along the bottom of the cliff lay rocks and boulders that over the eons had fallen as the cliff eroded. He found one the right size, and with much effort he rolled it over and over again until he fit it into the front of the entrance to the cavern. For extra caution he dug up samplings of cottonwoods and sycamores and transplanted them across the front of the alcove. They would grow fast and live for a hundred years, and they would drop seeds. Before many years, the area would be a dense grove.

The sun had set, and it was too late to venture back up the river. Besides, he was too weary to fight the current for the miles needed to go back past the town to his cabin on the bluff beyond. He sat on the large rock he had rolled in front of the cave entrance and leaned back against the cliff wall. *Just for a little while,* he thought. *Then I will go to the river and sleep in the dugout.* He closed his eyes and sleep was upon him.

A sound woke him. He blinked a few times and waited for his head to clear. The moon had not yet risen, so the sky was full. More stars than grains of sands on the beach. Abooksigun never tired of gazing into a beautiful night sky. A meteorite shot across the sky and the old man thought once more about Tecumseh—in The People's language, his name had meant The Shooting Star.

A rustling brought him to awareness. He stood slowly and waited. There it was, again, and now Abooksigun could see him—or, at least his yellow eyes. *Ah, it is thee, ayapia,* he thought. *Did you bring your brothers?*

Whether there was one wolf or more, the old man knew there would be no sudden attack. He quickly gathered some dead grass and small sticks that were close at hand, made a pile at the mouth of the alcove, reached into his pocket, and brought out his chert and steel. He held them low into the grass and with a few short strokes brought the sharp chert stone down onto the steel. Sparks flew and within a few seconds he had a small fire in the grass clump. He stacked small sticks, then larger ones. Within minutes he had a healthy fire. He knew wolves would not soon press into the light. Perhaps they wouldn't at all—they probably would not unless they had the rabid madness.

Abooksigun ventured out of the alcove to the edge of the light and gathered all the dead branches he could find. As he did so, the wolf backed farther into the shadows, his yellow eyes still watching. You will never attack straight on, Abooksigun thought. You would rather attack from behind, or from the sides. He glanced to the left. He could see another pair of eyes watching him and he found yet a third set of eyes watching him off to his right. *So, now we know, there are three of you.*

With his armload of branches, he backed into his alcove. With the cliff at his back and its walls wrapping around him, he was fairly protected. He was not afraid. He had lived with wolves his whole life. And, he had been born and raised a warrior—warriors do not fear battle or death.

He drew his knife from its sheaf, chose the two longest sticks from his woodpile, and sharpened the ends on both. He sat on the ground behind the fire. From this vantage point he could easily watch the wolf to his front and those on either side.

The old man was weary from the day's labor. His body yearned for the relief of sleep and he had to force it from his mind. *It will be a long night,* he thought. *I must keep the fire strong.* He said a prayer to the spirit Manitou and settled for the wait.

The moon rose now and cast its brightness. He could see the three wolves. *They are huge beasts,* he thought. *I, myself, cannot be much bigger.* The two on the sides sat. The one straight across from him in the edge of the brush stood, his tail wagging, his head held high, ears erect and his mouth open. *So,* the old man thought, *you will stay and fight tonight. It is well, ayapia, I am ready.*

An hour went by, and Abooksigun fed the fire. When next he did so, he saw the three wolves had ventured closer. When he built the fire a third time they had moved, again, just outside the circle of firelight. They all sat now, watching, waiting. *How much longer?* he wondered.

Sleep pressed him and he stood to make himself stay awake. He used the rest of his wood to build the fire for a last time. He was too tired to dance the hilenhenakawa, but he chanted the words of the war dance and spoke aloud the words that always preceded battle. "My brothers, the enemy is at hand. We must fight. Retreat would be disgraceful. We shall conquer if we are brave. The water will wash them away, the wind will blow them down, darkness will come upon them, and the earth will cover them."

Finally, the tired body forced its way back to the ground. His head slumped, and the motion jerked him back awake. The wolves were standing now. He placed his two spears on the ground next to him, one on each side of where he sat, and stuck his knife point-first into the ground so he could grasp it easily. He thought of his namesake, the wildcat. *We will see tonight which prevails,* he thought—*the wildcat or the wolf.*

He lowered his head as if asleep, luring them in, moving his eyes from side to side, watching the wolves inch in. He knew they would attack from the sides, never first from the front. With a sudden motion and snarl the wolf from the right leapt. At the same time Abooksigun grabbed a spear, raised it and caught the wolf in midair, piercing him through the throat. The weight of the falling wolf knocked him over and he scrambled to find the other spear on the ground.

The wolf from the left attacked, and his jaws grabbed the old man by the ankle and started to drag him face-down across the sand. Abooksigun found the other stick, twisted, and swung it off-balance. He struck the head of the wolf, making the beast release his grip with a yelp, then with all his strength he dug the point of the spear into the wild animal's side. The wolf cried and lumbered into the darkness, dragging the spear with it.

Panting, the old man rolled over and sat up. He slumped to catch his breath, but carefully watched the third wolf directly in front of him across the fire. He felt for his knife sticking up out of the sand, fitting the leather handle firmly into his hand, and smiled. *Come ayapia,* he thought, and he pulled the knife from the ground. *Come. Let us see if the wildcat can prevail.*

The wolf leapt straight through fire. Its tail hit the embers and sent a shower of sparks into the night sky. The weight of the animal knocked Abooksigun to the ground as the two fought. With one arm he wrestled to pin the wolf, and with downward motion he dug the point of his knife into the animal again and again, but the wolf was too strong for the old man. Its jaws finally found and closed on Abooksigun's throat. As darkness took him, the old man brought the knife one last time deep into the wolf's body, and the two—still locked in battle—became still.

Chapter 2

Monticello, White County, Indiana, June 1925

The four teenagers sat on the large limestone outcropping that overlooked the creek on the south edge of the Miller's farm. Billy Mac sat and looked at the water while the others encouraged him. He didn't really want to get in—it looked cold. And, besides, it wasn't even officially summer yet. But the water levels were low enough now. It had to be done and he was the one who had to do it.

Billy Mac Finch had just turned sixteen. Emmett Trentham, his best friend and confidante, was a year older. They had gravitated to each other at a young age—each was an only child and each had lost a parent when they were young. Billy Mac's mother had died from scarlet fever when he was a baby. Emmett had lost his father to the Great War. Like so many others, he had gone to Europe to fight the Germans. Like many others, he never came back—he had lost his life at the Battle of the Somme.

Billy Mac and Emmett were a contrast to each other. Billy Mac, in his short, stocky, disheveled, shy and quiet manner, admired the taller, good-looking Emmett with his quick wit and charm. While Billy Mac's awkward uncertainty caused him to hesitate, Emmett seemed to flow through life effortlessly. While Billy Mac struggled with his schoolwork, Emmett's natural curiosity and penchant for reading made him an authority on just about everything. He was maddening, sometimes. And, while Billy Mac approached life in general with caution, Emmett's humor and full-steam-ahead personality had gotten them into a jam more times than Billy Mac could remember. Emmett had a habit of flicking his eyebrows up and down anytime he had a mischievous idea.

Maddie Miller lived at the farm with her mother, grandfather—Doc Miller—and her companion, Boomer. She'd had the golden retriever since he was a six-week-old puppy. They were inseparable. Maddie had the habit of tilting her head with a smile to sweep the bangs away from her dark, flashing eyes. Billy Mac was glad Maddie and Emmett had finally acknowledged their affection for each other. It was easy to see why Emmett liked the smart, petite girl. Although they never excluded him, he couldn't help but feel like the odd man out sometimes.

Joseph Noble ran his father's blacksmith shop. He was admired by both the children and adults of Monticello. Work orders were always delivered flawlessly and ahead of schedule. It was amazing how he could work through the day of the shop and his white shirt above his leather apron remained spotless. Like others of Native American heritage, his tall, thin frame moved in a smooth and efficient manner. His jet-black hair hung to his eyes above an ever-present pearl-white smile.

"C'mon, Mackie," Emmett prodded Billy Mac.

"I know," Billy Mac grumbled. "I know." He kicked his shoes off.

Maddie sat beside him scratching Boomer's ears. Joseph took the coil of cotton well rope off his shoulder and handed one end to Billy Mac. He then wrapped the other end around a corner of the limestone jutting out of the ground and tied it securely.

"Okay, Mackie," Emmett instructed. "Tie it 'round your waist then grab hold. We'll lower you down."

Billy Mac silently did so, stood up, and nodded at them. "Okay. Here we go. Make sure you have a good grip."

He walked to the edge of the drop-off and looked down. There was a small ledge about ten feet down with the water about ten feet below that.

Last summer had been a flurry of adventure. They'd found a beautifully carved, ceremonial Indian pipe in a fallen-down cabin that had been built by Doc Miller's father—the first doctor in what was then a new territory—as a young man a hundred years prior. The ceremonial pipe had been given to the young doctor by an old Shawnee warrior one winter as payment for nursing him back from sickness.

They had shown the pipe to Doc Miller and the local librarian, Matilda Lee, who told them the legend of Tecumseh's lost gold. Then, an elderly Shawnee friend of Joseph's, Askuwheteau—the son of the warrior who had hidden the gold—had told them how carvings in the pipe would help locate the treasure. But it was too late. By that time, the pipe had been stolen by a renegade Indian, Ahote. On his deathbed, Askuwheteau told his young friends that Ahote was actually the estranged son he had disavowed many years prior because of his greed and cruel nature. Before he died, Askuwheteau also whispered to Billy Mac the interpretation of the carved pipe—the key to locate Tecumseh's legendary gold hoard.

While being chased down a dried-up creek bed by the renegade Ahote, Billy Mac had hidden in a small cave he'd found at the bottom of a limestone wall. Ahote found Billy Mac and dragged him out of the cave. Billy Mac had hung onto a rock in the cave floor but the rock had come loose and Ahote had him, choking him in the creek bed to get the information he wanted. Doc Miller snuck up behind them as they brawled and knocked Ahote unconscious with his cane. A fierce thunderstorm had caused a flash flood in the creek and neither the pipe nor Ahote was ever seen, again. Did the renegade drown, or did he get away? No one knew.

The next day as the four young friends pieced all of the information together, it all made sense. The cave Billy Mac had found to hide in was the location of the gold. The smooth rock he'd held onto while Ahote dragged him out into the creek bed had been a bar of gold embedded in the cave floor. Flooding kept them from going back into the creek, then autumn turned into winter. They would have to wait until spring and low water levels to venture back into that cave. The four friends vowed to keep the secret to themselves until they could do so. So now, today was the day. Billy Mac was going back down that limestone wall and into the cave to find the gold.

Billy Mac tied the rope around his waist, sat down, and worked his way over the rock ledge. Holding onto the rope, he bounced off the rock face with his feet as Emmett and Joseph lowered him. *Would that rock—or gold bar—still be in the sandy bottom of the cave floor?* he wondered. *Why wouldn't it be?*

"Almost there," he yelled up at the others. *Here we go. Jeez, the water is cold, he thought.* His feet found the bottom of the creek—he was down. The water was waist high.

"I made it!" he yelled again. "I'm gonna work my way inside. Don't let go of that rope!"

He worked his way to the small fissure that formed the mouth of the little cave, turned sideways, and worked his way in.

The memories of his battle against Ahote flooded back. He pictured himself lying on the cave floor fighting and kicking as Ahote dragged him out of the cave into the creek bed.

I was lying...just...about...here, he thought. He stooped, reached through the water, and felt around the sandy floor. Then, his heart jumped. He felt the rock. Slowly he lifted the heavy object out of the water. Even in the dim light of the cave he could see the soft glow of the gold.

"I got it!" he yelled. "Oh my gosh I got it! I'm coming out. When I tug on the rope bring me back up!"

A few minutes later, Billy Mac was back at the top of the creek bank. He sat soaking wet on the limestone boulder, the bar of gold cradled in his lap.

"Oh, my!" Maddie said, somewhat breathless. "So, it's true—it's all true." She cocked her head to brush her black bangs from her eyes as she peered down at the grinning Billy Mac.

"Mackie, good job!" Emmett whispered, his eyes fixated on the gold bar.

"I don't believe it," Joseph murmured. "I just don't believe it. All of those stories, for all of those years. I just never thought it could be true."

Billy Mac passed the bar to Joseph, who eventually passed it on to Emmett and Maddie. They each took turns turning it over and weighing the bar up and down in their hands. Although it was small in size, it was very heavy.

"What do we do now?" Maddie asked. The four friends looked at each other.

"I hafta go back down," Billy Mac answered. "We hafta get the rest of it."

"Right," Emmett echoed. "There's supposed to be two hundred bars, total. We can't bring them all up here and stack them up out here in the open for anyone to see, but let's count what's down there. Then, we'll decide what to do with it. You okay to go back down there, Mackie?"

Billy Mac looked at his friends, nodded, and scooted back to the edge of the rock. "Okay," he said. "Here we go."

The boys lowered him back down. Once he reached bottom, he worked his way back through the fissure in the rock face and stood in the small cave for a minute to let his eyes adjust to the dim light.

Then, he squatted and duck-walked all around the cave wall, feeling the sandy floor as he sloshed through the water. Nothing.

"You okay, Mackie?" he heard Emmett yell. "How many have you got so far?"

"I'm fine," he yelled back. "Just hold on a minute. I'm lookin' 'round."

He squatted and crisscrossed the cave, running his hands back and forth and all around on the sandy floor. Still nothing.

"Mackie?" Emmett yelled again.

"Hold on!" *How could there be nothing here?* he thought.

After several minutes—and repeated yells to his friends to hold on—he stood up and worked his way through the opening back out into the creek bed.

"Okay. Bring me back up!"

The four sat on the rock shaking their heads.

"How can there be nothing else?" Emmett repeated. "It doesn't make sense."

"It sure doesn't," Joseph agreed. "Why would there just be the one bar?"

"It must've all been here, sometime," Billy Mac said.

"Maybe it was all there and then they moved it all somewhere else," Maddie said. "Maybe they accidentally left it behind when they carried it out. Maybe one just fell from the stack. Or, maybe they just dropped one while they carried the rest out and didn't realize it."

"I don't see how they could," Emmett said. "It's not like you would carry a stack in your arms all at the same time and one could fall off. You have to move these one at a time, they're so heavy."

"Maybe whoever moved it left one on purpose without anyone else knowing, so he could come back and get it for himself," Billy Mac thought out loud.

"That doesn't make sense, either," Joseph said. "Remember, Askuwheteau talked of how that small band of warriors took vows. They were committed to Tecumseh and his cause. They weren't in it for themselves. There was no greed among them. They were honorable."

"I was so sure we would find it," Emmett sighed. His disappointment was palpable. "I was just so sure."

Maddie stood up. "But we have this," she hoisted the gold bar. "This is something. What do we do now?"

"I have to get back to the shop," Joseph said and stood up. "I'll give you guys a ride back to town in the wagon." He nodded to Emmett and Billy Mac.

"Yeah," Billy Mac said. "I've got chores to do."

"Yeah, I promised Mom I'd help her at The Strand, and I'm supposed to see someone about a summer job down at the dam they're building on the river south of town," Emmett said.

"But, what do we do about this?" Maddie asked again. She handed the gold bar to Emmett.

"I think it's time we talked to a few other people about it, now that we know this is real," Emmett said. "I think we need to talk to Ms. Lee and Skinner. And, I think we need to include Billy Mac's dad."

Matilda Lee was the local librarian. She and Principal Skinner had become allies to the four friends the previous summer when the adventure of the tomahawk pipe and search for the gold began. Billy Mac's father was the town sheriff.

Everyone nodded in agreement.

"Maddie, you usually come to town on Saturday with your mom for groceries," Emmett said. "How about if we all meet Saturday at the library at noon? I'll get word to Ms. Lee and Skinner. Billy Mac, you can check with your dad." He held a hand out, palm down. "Agreed?"

"Agreed!" the other three echoed and stacked their hands on top of his.

"What do we do with that?" Maddie asked again and pointed to the gold bar Emmett was holding.

Emmett handed it to Billy Mac. "You keep it for now. You found it."

Billy Mac nodded. He reached for his ever-present backpack, opened it, put the gold bar inside, then buckled it back up.

"Okay," he said. "Let's go."

They walked across the field, through the rows of the tender green corn shoots, with Boomer bounding toward the farmhouse in front of them.

Chapter 3

Billy Mac heard a faint voice in the distance and walked toward it. A familiar voice, he thought. He squinted in the poor light and waved his hands in front of his face trying to see through the dense fog.

He heard the voice again and slowly walked along the grassy lane. I've been here before, *he thought.*

"Come, my neekanhuh," the voice beckoned.

Billy Mac stopped and peered through the haze. "Askuwheteau?" he called. "Is that you?"

"Come." The voice grew fainter.

"Askuwheteau! Askuwheteau!" Billy Mac called back and started walking again, faster.

"Come…" The voice faded away.

"Askuwheteau! Don't leave!"

Billy Mac woke up. He lay in bed, panting, catching his breath, then shook his head a few times to clear his head. Jeez! It had happened again. Such strange dreams. They were so real.

He sat up on the side of his bed, pulled on his trousers, socks, and shoes, reached for his backpack, and walked into the kitchen. His father was long gone—he had early rounds to make.

Billy Mac sat at the table, pulled his sketchpad and some pencils out of the backpack. *Best to try and capture it on paper while it was fresh on his mind,* he thought. He ate a quick muffin and drank a glass of milk from the icebox while he sketched.

Fifteen minutes later he put the sketchpad and pencils into the backpack, walked to the sink, pumped some water, and washed his face. He grabbed two metal buckets from the counter, pushed his way through the screen door, turned, and caught the door with his foot so the spring wouldn't slam it closed, then made his daily trek to the chicken yard and henhouses.

He'd done this hundreds of times—didn't even have to think. It was automatic. He put one bucket on the ground and stooped to go into the first henhouse. He made his way up one side, reaching under plump hens to pull out warm brown eggs and put them softly into the bucket. *Why would I have those weird dreams?* he thought. He turned and walked down the other side repeating the motions. *Why would I dream about Askuwheteau?* He stooped again, went out of the henhouse, put the bucket of eggs on the ground, reached for the empty bucket, went into the second henhouse, and repeated the regimen.

Billy Mac carried both buckets of eggs back into the house, catching the screen door with his backside. He pumped water into each bucket, set them on the counter, then pumped water into a third bucket. He stuck a kitchen match, lit a candle, and placed it on the counter next to the buckets and the stack of empty cartons.

One by one he took each egg, sloshed it around in its bucket, and then rubbed the fluff and debris off it. Then he took it, washed it off a second time in the bucket of clean water, and dried it off with a washrag. Before putting it into a carton he bent over and passed it back and forth in front of the candle flame to look for cracks in the translucent eggshells. He rarely found any.

Done with the eggs, Billy Mac did his other routine chores—the stove box had plenty of wood and corncobs, and the lanterns in the house each had plenty of kerosene. It would be nice once the new dam on the river was working and they got electricity, like they had down at the jailhouse. They'd be one of the first houses to get it, since his father was the sheriff and needed a phone. Then they could get rid of the kerosene lamps.

He checked the icebox. It needed a block of ice. He'd stop by the mill over at the train tracks and ask for one to be brought over. He usually liked to stop by the mill. It was a good place to escape from the summer heat. Fresh ground grains filled the air with the sugar-sweet smell of molasses, and old farmers loitered in a corner of the office waiting for their turn to beat the winner at the last game of checkers. They were fun to watch as they poked fun at each other. He wouldn't have time to stop and watch today, though. He needed to get to the library.

Last, he went to the front room, reached up to open the glass panel on the wall clock, took the key, and wound the spring a few turns. Then, he went back to the kitchen, picked up the stack of egg cartons, made his way outside, and turned down the bluff toward town. He'd have just enough time to get the eggs to Morris's Market and then get to the library to meet everyone.

He always enjoyed this walk. He looked down the bluff at the Tippecanoe River. The mist had just about burned off the water. He saw a few fishing boats, but it was mostly quiet.

Billy Mac dropped the eggs off, left the market, made a quick stop at the mill to order a block of ice to be delivered, and then headed for the library. Conscious of the weight of the gold bar in his backpack, he thought about Ms. Lee and Skinner. He liked them both. For as long as he could remember he'd been a victim of Ms. Lee's kind, good-natured teasing to visit the library and read more. He just didn't have much of an interest in it like Emmett did. Billy Mac shook his head thinking about Emmett. Emmett the reader. Emmett the authority on everything. Emmett had started reading everything he could get his hands on when they were younger. He'd missed a whole year of school from illness and reading helped him pass the time. He'd started reading and just never stopped. Ms. Lee always had new books waiting for him every few weeks.

And Skinner. *Principal* Skinner. He'd come to town from Lafayette a year prior as Monticello's principal for the new schoolhouse. Their first impression of him was not good after he had unintentionally embarrassed Maddie at a social held on his behalf to welcome him to town. Emmett's harebrained scheme to make amends comically backfired. But, after that rocky start the boys soon found him to be a friend and ally in their adventures. Billy Mac liked him, even if he couldn't always understand the fancy way he talked. It was a good thing Emmett was always around to interpret.

Billy Mac walked into the library, the little bell above the door tingling. *It is nice in here,* he thought. *Nice and quiet, and cool. Nice to get out of the heat.*

"Back here, Mackie," Emmett called to him.

"Please turn the sign for me, Billy Mac," Ms. Lee's voice asked.

Billy Mac reached up, turned the sign in the window from "Open" to "Closed," and then made his way through a row of bookshelves to the back of the library. He found everyone there waiting on him, sitting at a large harvest table. Emmett sat next to Maddie, of course, with Maddie rubbing Boomer's head; Joseph with his ever-present smile; Principal Skinner; Ms. Lee; and his father, the sheriff, with quizzical looks on their faces.

Ms. Lee, an attractive middle-aged woman, looked the librarian. Her hair was wound in a bundle on top of her head with a pencil stuck through to hold it up, and reading glasses hung from a silver chain around her neck.

Principal Skinner was tall in a heavy frame. The boys had never seen him when he wasn't wearing a three-piece suit with his shirt buttoned tight all the way up into his neck. Tortoise shell glasses sat on a sharp, hawkish nose. He presented himself as the consummate academic he was.

Billy Mac's father, in his sheriff's uniform, always offered a calm, assuring and capable presence. Billy Mac admired his father and the two enjoyed an enviable father-son relationship.

"Hey, Pa," Billy Mac said and sat down next to the sheriff. His father patted him on the back.

"Well, well," Principal Skinner said, his hands on the table, tapping his fingertips together. He had a funny habit of repeating words.

"So, what's going on?" his father asked the group, looking from one to the other.

"Not sure, but it's never dull with this troupe," Ms. Lee smiled. "Who wants to start?"

Billy Mac looked at his friends. They looked back and forth at each other. Finally, Billy Mac nodded to Emmett.

"Well," Emmett started, "remember last year, all the things that happened? The tomahawk pipe we'd found in that cabin out on the Millers' farm? Ahote stealing it from Billy Mac's backpack, and the fight we had with him that night out at the creek? How we went to Askuwheteau's cabin to get it back after he'd stolen it back from Ahote? The fight they had, and all that?"

"Well, sure," the sheriff said. "Of course, we remember. Ahote fought with Askuwheteau before chasing you boys down into the creek bed. He'd have really hurt Billy Mac, too, if Doc Miller hadn't come to the rescue. That bad storm blew in and all the flooding it caused. Everyone was saddened that Askuwheteau didn't survive the ordeal."

"And, we are all aware said pipe was irrevocably lost in said torrent. Unfortunate, unfortunate," Skinner said, tapping his fingertips together. "I should have liked to have been given the opportunity to examine the artifact in detail. You'll recall I could only interpret one-half of the carved communiqué as we only had one-half to view via the rather exquisite rendering young Mr. Finch so aptly portrayed in his tablet."

"You all believed that tomahawk pipe was to have been a map to gold which Tecumseh's warriors were supposed to have hidden," Ms. Lee said. "We all know that. I'm still not sure I believe in that old legend despite everything that took place last summer. But I know that's what you all believed, as did Askuwheteau and Ahote."

"Well, there's something we—the four of us—never told you," Emmett said. "That night when we'd finally gotten back to Askuwheteau's cabin to check on him, he was hurt real bad. Remember we put him on his bed?"

"I do," the sheriff said. "He was injured pretty badly, very badly for a man of his advanced age. He didn't want us to try to take him to Doc's, so we tried to make him as comfortable as possible. He died shortly after."

"Right," Emmett agreed. "But, remember right before he died, he called to Billy Mac?"

"Vaguely," the sheriff said. He turned to look at his son.

Billy Mac fidgeted, never comfortable to be the center of attention. He looked at his friends, who nodded for him to continue.

"Askuwheteau told me what the message on the pipe was," he said. "The whole thing. The whole message."

The adults straightened in their chairs, speechless.

"It was enough. Maddie realized what—where—he was talking about. He told us where to look," Billy Mac said. "It was right there, at Maddie's farm, the same spot we'd been camping at." He looked at Maddie to continue.

"There is a limestone outcropping that goes all the way down the face of the creek bank," Maddie said. "At the bottom is a crack in the rock—it opens into a small cave. The same one Billy Mac tried to hide in last year from Ahote."

"But, why now?" Ms. Lee asked. "Why are we talking about it now? All of this started a year ago."

"Last year when this all happened, there was bad flooding, just as the sheriff remembers," Joseph said. "We couldn't get back down into that creek bed. Then school started, the weather turned bad, and there was just never a chance. Believe me, we wanted to investigate, but we never could. Winter came. Then spring rains kept the creek too deep with a fairly strong current."

"And?" the sheriff asked.

"A couple days ago we were finally able to check it out," Emmett continued. "The water was finally low enough to stand in. We lowered Billy Mac down, but kept him tethered. He was finally able to get inside that little cave."

"And?" the sheriff repeated.

"Show them, Mackie," Emmett said matter-of-factly.

Billy Mac looked at the faces all looking at him. He turned—twisting to get both hands deep into the backpack hanging on the back of his chair—pulled out the heavy gold bar, leaned forward, and with a loud clunk it slipped from his hands and dropped into the middle of the table.

The silence was deafening.

Billy Mac looked at Emmett, Maddie, and Joseph, who were beaming. Then at his father, Ms. Lee and Principal Skinner, all of whom wore expressions of disbelief.

Billy Mac broke the silence. "Sorry, Ms. Lee," he said. "It's kinda heavy."

"Extraordinary," Principal Skinner said as he leaned forward for a closer look through the glasses on the end of his nose. "Simply extraordinary."

Ms. Lee shook her head, expressionless, gazing at the gold bar. Years of disbelief washed away by the reality of what she saw.

The sheriff reached forward and picked it up. "There are more of these?" he asked as he examined the gold bar.

"No, sir," Billy Mac answered. "It's a small cave. I crisscrossed every bit of it. There's nothing else down there."

Ms. Lee came out of her stupor. "According to your legend, there were supposed to be two hundred of these, right?" she asked, pointing at the gold bar.

"Right," Maddie answered. "That's what the old Indian brave told Gramps' father all those years ago. That they buried—or hid—two hundred bars of gold."

"But that would mean…," the sheriff started, weighing the heavy bar up and down in his hands. "That would mean…how much total…if each were the same as this?"

"The standard to melt gold into bars," Emmett offered, "was eight inches long, three inches wide, and two inches high. Each about twenty-five pounds."

"Which would equate to what?" the sheriff asked, still looking at the gold.

"Five thousand pounds, or eighty thousand ounces," Emmett answered. "At twenty dollars an ounce."

"Extraordinary," Principal Skinner repeated. "Simply extraordinary."

The sheriff turned it over, then from side to side as he studied it. "No markings on it. Just some scratches." He placed the gold bar back on the table, again with a clunk. "What are you going to do with it? What's your next step?"

"We're not quite sure," Joseph answered. "Our goal was to find the gold and then turn it over to a collected council of The People. They could perhaps provide guidance on how best to use it among the tribes. Maybe it could be used to help train tribal members for jobs or offer scholarships for education. Maybe they could also find a way to preserve and promote their cultures. According to Askuwheteau, their vow was to only use the gold to help The People regain what they had lost to whites. Prophetstown had members from many tribes—the Miami's, which my family belongs to, Shawnees, Weas, Potawatomis, and another dozen from across the country. We were hopeful they could work together and find common agreement on the best ways to use the gold for the betterment of all The People."

"A worthy thought," Ms. Lee nodded.

"But, one bar of gold isn't going to do much for anyone," Emmett said. "We want to keep looking for the rest of the gold, but we haven't had enough time yet to decide what to do next."

"Joseph," the sheriff said. "Since you and your family are a member of the Miami nation, why don't you write to your elders? They're in Peru, Indiana, aren't they? That's not too far from here. Invite them to send a representative to meet with all of you. You can then share with them all you know—and what you have—so far. Maybe they can help. They might have additional information you all might find useful to continue your search. Bring your letter to me, and I'll mail it from the sheriff's office with a note of my own to assure them it's not a waste of their time."

"That would be great, Pa," Billy Mac said. "Joseph, what do you think?"

"I agree," Joseph said. "It sure can't hurt anything. At this point, we have nothing else to go on."

"Sheriff, can you keep that locked up in your office for now?" Emmett asked, pointing to the gold bar.

"You bet," he said as he picked it up. He looked at the four friends and patted Billy Mac on the back. "I'm proud of all of you. But, two things, if Ms. Lee and the principal agree. First, the fewer the people that know about this the better. I understand if you want to share it with your parents and your grandfather, Maddie. Joseph, you may want to share it with your father, as well. But I wouldn't tell anyone beyond that. Second, last summer got kind of dangerous for all of you. You should have let me know what was going on. Promise you'll let me know if anything even remotely happens while you keep your search up?"

"Promise!" the four answered together.

"Ms. Lee? Principal?" the sheriff said. "Anything you'd like to add?"

"Sounds like a plan to me," Ms. Lee said with a smile. "I'm sure Principal Skinner would agree that we are both available at any time to help however we can."

"Most assuredly," Principal Skinner agreed, tapping his fingertips together. "Most assuredly!"

Chapter 4

A short while later the four teenagers sat on the benches in the shade of the sycamore outside of Joseph's blacksmith shop. Boomer had plopped down on the cool earth at the bottom of the tree trunk.

"So," Joseph said. "I'll figure it out tonight. We get letters from the nation every now and then. Father keeps them all. I'll go through them and determine who to write to. The members of the tribal council are always listed. Then, I'll take my letter to the sheriff in the morning."

"What do we do in the meantime?" Billy Mac asked. "There's really nothing for us to go on, is there?"

"Not really, Mackie," Emmett said. "Besides, I got that job for the summer working at the construction site for the new Oakdale dam. Between helping Ma at The Strand and working at the dam, I'm gonna be pretty busy."

"Me, too," Joseph said. He jerked a thumb to the area at the far end of their shop. They could hear someone clanking around. "Now that Father spends most of his time working on autos, I've got all the blacksmith work to do on my own."

"Ma's keeping me busy," Maddie said. "My cousin Becky, from Indianapolis, is going to stay with us all of next school year while her parents are away. I'm in charge of cleaning out a room and fixing it up for her. And, that means more canning and preserving than normal. She's so sweet, though. Can't wait for her to come!"

"Look who we got here," Joseph said, nodding out at the street.

Gus and his gang were walking up the path. They'd unknowingly been a part of the story last summer. Ten-year-old Gus and his troupe looked to Joseph and Emmett as mentors, always soliciting them for advice.

Gus didn't look his usual self. His hair was combed and slicked back with pomade, his patched overalls looked like they'd been pressed, his shirt was clean—and he had shoes on, as did most of his followers.

"Gus, boys," Joseph nodded at them. "How's everyone today?"

"Not too good," Gus said and pulled at his buttoned-up shirt collar. "Wonderin' if'n you can help."

"Try to," Joseph smiled. "Everyone is looking pretty nice. What are ya'll cleaned up for?"

"Gotta go to church!" Gus mumbled, kicking the ground. The boys behind him all grumbled.

"On a Saturday?" Maddie asked.

"Vacation Bible School," Emmett answered. "You boys gotta go for the whole week?" he asked the gang.

"Yeah! Fer the whole week!" Gus cried. "Every darn day fer a whole blasted week!"

Gus looked at Emmett and Joseph. "You gotta help us. Ain't there no way we kin get outta doin' it?"

Maddie put a hand to her mouth and tried to suppress a giggle.

"Well," Emmett said and dramatically peered into the distance, rubbing his chin. He looked at Billy Mac and flicked his eyebrows up and down a few times.

"Emmo," Billy Mac cautioned. Every time Gus and his gang looked for help, Emmett's solutions usually got them in trouble.

"Let me think...," Emmett continued.

"Emmo!" Billy Mac cut him off.

"Okay, Mackie. Okay." Emmett raised his hands in defense. He looked at Gus. "Sorry, buddy. Nothing I can think of. Think you're going to have to tough this one out."

Gus hung his head. It was a fate worse than death. "Gosh darn it! Jiminy! C'mon, guys!"

Billy Mac watched the troupe shuffle back down to the street and turn toward town. Maddie giggled out loud and Joseph chuckled.

"It would have been easy," Emmett said with his classic mischievous smile on his face. "I could have gotten them out of it."

"Yeah, but they wouldn't have been able to sit down for a week after their moms and dads got done with 'em," Billy Mac said.

"Might have been worth it, to them, though," Emmett said. "Can't imagine that crew having to sit inside for a whole week all trussed up in this heat."

"Okay. I've got to go," Maddie said and stood up. "Ma's waiting for me at the market. How will we know when to get back together?"

Joseph watched Gus and his boys turn a corner in the distance. "I know," he said. "When I hear back from the nation, I'll send Gus to get word to all of you. I'll give them some old horseshoes from the scrap pile. That'll make them happy. Agreed?" he said and put his hand out in front of him.

"Agreed," the others echoed, and all put their hands out on top of his.

Billy Mac lay on his cot and looked up into the still night. It was fairly routine for him and Emmett to sleep on their back porches during the summer heat. Sometimes they slept over at Emmett's, sometimes at his house.

Billy Mac liked summer nights. The cooler breeze brought relief and the sweet smell of Johnson grass and honeysuckle. It was quiet. The chickens were all settled in the henhouse; crickets faintly chirped in unison.

"Emmo?" Billy Mac called.

"Yeah?"

"What will we do?"

"What d'ya mean, Mackie?"

"About the gold. What do we do now? We got nothin' to go on."

"It's okay."

"What d'ya mean, it's okay?"

"Look," Emmett said and rolled over on his cot to face Billy Mac. "We made a great breakthrough. We found out that the gold really does exist. It's real. Right? So, we take it one step at a time. I think your pa had a good idea. We'll follow that for now. If that doesn't turn anything up, we'll think of something else. One step at a time. Okay?"

"Yeah," Billy Mac said. "Okay. Night, Emmo."

"Night, Mackie."

Billy Mac turned, laid on his back, and closed his eyes. The soft, steady chirping of the crickets lolled him into a slumber, and he dozed off.

"Neekanhuh," the voice called.

Billy Mac peered through the fog and called back. "Hello?"

"Come, neekanhuh. Come sit with me."

"Askuwheteau? Is that you?" Billy Mac called. "I'm coming!"

He walked slowly down a familiar grassy lane, careful with each step, the fog was so thick. The hillside jutted up on the right side of the lane and was covered in trees.

"Hello!" Billy Mac called. "Askuwheteau?"

"Yes, neekanhuh," the voice called. "Yes. Come and sit. We must talk."

The lane curved to the right. Billy Mac followed it slowly. He could barely make out the outlines of the cabin now through the mist.

"I'm coming," Billy Mac called. "Wait for me!"

Billy Mac woke up, startled and bothered. He blinked a few times and shook his head to bring himself back to reality. *Oh, my gosh! It was so real. Why do I keep having that dream?* he wondered.

He rolled over, wanting to talk to Emmett about these dreams he kept having. But he could hear the slow breathing of deep sleep from the dark lump that was Emmett lying on his cot.

Billy Mac rolled onto his back, wide awake now, and looked up at the stars. It was going be a long night.

Chapter 5

The men sat around a campfire in the middle of a grove of trees. Ahote poked at the fire with a stick.

"What yer sayin' is, you want me to leave," he snarled at the other four men sitting around the fire.

"What we're saying," the leader of the four hobos said, "is you don't follow the Code. We don't steal from each other. We keep ourselves clean and present ourselves as gentlemen the way the Code was writ. We show respect for the people and places we pass through. We all do our share and help each other."

Ahote looked at the other three faces around the campfire. They all nodded in agreement. "So, you want me to leave?" he asked again with a sneer.

"Yeah," the hobo leader said. "We want you to leave. Now. And, don't come back. We'll be a watchin'."

Ahote looked at them for a long moment and then spat on the ground in a show of disrespect. He took his time to stand up, then slowly made his way through the trees and up the embankment to the railroad tracks. He paused for a minute to decide which way to go. He rubbed through his matted hair and then scratched his grimy, unshaven chin. *That's all right,* he thought. *I don't need them boys anymore. I lived off 'em long enough. And, to Hell with the Code.*

He reached into the one pocket of his ratty clothes that didn't have a hole it in, pulled out a half-empty pint bottle of cheap whiskey, pulled the cork with his teeth, and spat it out back down the embankment into the tall grass. He gulped the rest of the brown liquor so that it burned the back of his throat, wiped his mouth with the back of a dirty shirtsleeve, then threw the empty bottle onto a rail so it shattered dramatically. Then he turned and walked slowly through the night toward the glow in the sky of the nearest town.

What to do and where to go? Lately he'd been thinking about going home—back to Indiana. He'd been out west for almost year. *Would that be long enough?* he wondered. Maybe long enough for those kids to have found what they'd all been looking for? Maybe his father—Askuwheteau—would have helped them find it.

The thought of those kids and his father brought a rush of anger. Damn that old man. Why did his father always refuse to let him in on the secret? Well, if they'd found it, maybe he could find a way to get some of it—there were ways, if you didn't care about what you did and who you did it to. And, if they hadn't found it, well, he had a score to settle with some of 'em anyway. *Why not go?* he shrugged in the still night. He had nothing better to do, and no place better to be. He wasn't sure how he'd hang around town without someone recognizing him, but he'd figure it out.

He looked up at the stars to get a bearing, then turned around and headed east. It would be sun-up in a few hours. He could hustle some food in the next town and think out his plan.

A couple of hours later he could see the town across the river. He bent down and put his ear to the rail to make sure no train was coming, then continued on the narrow bridge. You had to be careful—if you got caught walking on a bridge when a train plowed through, there was no room for you to get out of the way. You'd have to jump. And, the river was a long way down.

As he neared town, he looked on trees, signs, and rocks for a symbol. Hobos always left a clue as to what type of town a fellow hobo was walking into. Then he saw it. To anyone else, it was just scratching on a boulder at the bottom of the rail bed—an upside-down U with a solid circle in the middle of it. To a fellow hobo it meant, "Authorities on alert in this town." Not friendly. He'd have to be careful.

At the edge of town he looked for more markings. There it was on a signpost. A circle with an arrow pointing. "Go this way." He followed until he saw another directing him up a street, then another down another street into a neighborhood. Then he saw what he was looking for carved into a tree—a stick figure of a woman, a large triangle, and three small triangles. To Ahote it read, "A kind lady lives here. Tell a pitiful story." Well, he could certainly do that. He could lie with the best of them. If she were a widow woman, she'd be an easy mark.

Two hours later he'd been fed and washed and had two pairs of clothing. The widow had correctly surmised Ahote to be the same size as her dear departed Clarence. She was only too happy to help a fellow Christian get home to bury his loving father. His bindle sack full with the second pair of clothes and enough food for a couple days, Ahote in a very courtly manner bid her thanks and blessings and then headed for the tracks.

He skulked around the railyard waiting for an eastbound and smiled at his success with the widow. He'd gotten rather good at performing. He could effectively pull it off—the benefit of riding the rails a few years back with a hobo named Stan who had worked the Vaudeville stages.

That's it! Before he got to Indiana, he'd be a new person. He could cut his hair, dye it if needed. He knew how to carry himself to appear larger or smaller and heavier or lighter. He still had the stage spectacles Stan had given him—wire frames with fake lenses in them. Ahote smiled. All he had to do was think of who he wanted to be and what his story was. They'd never know, until it was too late.

Chapter 6

Billy Mac and Emmett sat in the shade of the gazebo on the corner of the courthouse lawn waiting for Maddie. Like most Saturdays, Maddie and her mother would be in town to shop and pick up supplies.

Saturday mornings brought a beehive of activity to the usually sleepy town square. Even though most offices in the courthouse were closed, there were still people coming and going. The striking structure always reminded Billy Mac of what he thought a castle must look like with its thick limestone block wall and beautifully sculpted arched windows, doorways, and turrets. Four large clocks on each side of the magnificent bell tower showed it to be almost noon.

Billy Mac looked at the shops around the square. He could see girls sitting at the soda counter in the apothecary—the soda jerk was a handsome young fellow. The lunch crowd rotated in and out of the diner. A father dragged a reluctant boy into the barbershop. A wagon drove out of the livery, the driver snapping the reins. The bank was closed on Saturday, so there was no traffic there. But there were always people outside The Strand reading handbills to see what acts and picture shows were coming to town.

It had been three uneventful weeks since they'd all met at the library, except for the Fourth of July, which was fun as normal. Red, white, and blue banners still hung around the town square. It had come and gone in all its usual glory, the one time each year when all the county folks converged on the small town all at once. Horse-drawn wagons, along with a few autos, had lined all the streets that branched off the town square. The swell of the people imbibed with the promise of celebration was always electric. The parade was followed by picnics and games in the park. The town band in their regalia played under the bandstand, with well-deserved accolades to ninety-year-old Vidalia Bellew on the tuba. At sundown, fireworks launched from a barge on the river. Smoke from the black powder hung on the water and drifted up the shoreline into the park, thick as fog. The skyrockets were always Billy Mac's favorite. Watching them had reminded him of how last summer's mystery was just getting heated up on the Fourth.

Billy Mac hadn't seen Emmett much for the past few weeks. Billy Mac had been busy tending the chickens to take eggs to the market, keeping the garden weeded and helping out at the sheriff's office with some light chores. Emmett still helped his ma at The Strand whenever he could, and his new job working on the construction of Oakdale Dam south of the city kept him busy. When Emmett had had a few free evenings, he'd gone out to see Maddie at the farm. Emmett always asked Billy Mac to go with him, but he'd make excuses not to. He felt strange sometimes hanging out with them when Emmett and Maddie found a little time to visit with each other. His two friends would never leave him out on his own. It would hurt their feelings if they knew he purposely avoided them sometimes. His exclusion was of his own making, self-imposed.

They'd all gotten word to meet at Joseph's shop at lunchtime; thus, the two of them waited for Maddie before walking over.

"Here she comes," said Emmett.

Maddie waved as she and Boomer crossed the street to where they were sitting.

"Hey, guys," she called. A picnic basket hung in the crook of her arm.

"Whatcha got, Maddie?" Billy Mac asked as she and Boomer walked up.

"The usual," she answered. She tilted her head and brushed a wisp of her dark hair out of her brown eyes, then traded smiles with Emmett.

"Ready?" Emmett asked as he stood up.

"Yup!" Billy Mac answered.

They walked to the corner of the square then turned toward the blacksmith shop. A few blocks later they found Joseph, still in his leather apron, sitting on the bench in the shade of the sycamore out front.

Maddie spread a red and white checkered tablecloth on the ground while everyone exchanged good mornings, then put the picnic basket in the middle as she, Emmett, and Billy Mac sat on the corners. Boomer found his cool patch of earth on the north side of the tree trunk and plopped down, belly to the ground.

"What's up, Joseph?" Emmett took the lead and asked.

Joseph pulled a letter out of his leather apron and laid it on the bench.

"I heard back from the nation," he said.

"Good news?" Billy Mac asked as Maddie handed him a plate. "They interested?"

"Greatly interested," Joseph answered. He moved from the bench to sit at the edge of the tablecloth. He also took a plate from Maddie. "They are sending someone from their council, an elder named Taregan. The letter says we can expect him anytime during the current moon cycle, which means anytime in the four weeks." He reached into the picnic basket and pulled out a piece of fried chicken.

"So that's it, then?" Emmett mumbled. He swallowed and wiped a napkin across his mouth. "Nothing else in the letter?" he said.

"Nope," Joseph answered.

"Well, I guess it's something," Maddie said. "But I guess we just wait, if there's nothing else."

"I got somethin' I need to talk about," Billy Mac fidgeted. He hesitated, remembering he was the one last summer who thought he was seeing ghosts, which turned out not to be the case. He'd taken a lot of ribbing from Emmett for it.

"Well, Mackie?" Emmett asked. "What is it?"

Billy Mac took a deep breath. Normally when bothered by something he'd kick at the ground with his toe. Since he was sitting, he turned away from the blanket and poked at the ground with a stick.

"I've been having some weird dreams—about Askuwheteau." He looked around at his friends, who all just stared back in silence.

Five minutes later he had told them about the recurring dream, how each time he'd gotten a little farther down the lane, a little closer to the cabin, the voice was calling to him a little louder and clearer.

He waited for someone to say something. "Well?" he asked, a little annoyed. "What d'ya think?"

"Not sure, Mackie...," Emmett said slowly, shaking his head. "I don't know. Swear I don't."

Billy Mac fought to contain a slight smile. *Well, that's something, at least,* he thought. Not often Emmett doesn't have an answer for something.

"Joseph," Maddie started, "is it possible Askuwheteau's spirit is trying to reach out to Billy Mac?"

Joseph was looking at Billy Mac with an incredulous look on his face. He leaned forward, squinted, and looked deeply into Billy Mac's eyes.

Billy Mac, startled, sat up straight, leaned back away from Joseph a little, looked questioningly at Maddie and Emmett and then back to Joseph.

"It's possible," Joseph said softly as he leaned in even closer to Billy Mac, "But..."

"But...what?" Maddie asked.

"But I am not aware that happens outside The People," Joseph said slowly, still looking deeply into Billy Mac's eyes. "It might, but I'm just not aware of it. The spirit of a guardian can sometimes communicate with one of The People. But it takes much effort for one to attempt a vision quest." He backed away and looked around at his friends. "And, I am not aware of a spirit reaching out to a person—I am only aware of it working the other way around. A person, with much preparation and effort, attempts to communicate with their guardian spirit through a vision quest."

"Are you telling me," Billy Mac asked, rather shaken up, "this might be real? This might really be happening?"

"Of course it's happening," Emmett said. "You're having those dreams, aren't you?"

"I know I'm having the dreams, Emmo!" Billy Mac shot back. "But dreams are one thing. The spirit of a dead person reaching out to me is somethin' else!"

"Relax, Mackie," Emmett said. "I'm just saying, maybe it's something to go on. There's nothing scary about it. Askuwheteau was a friend, and he'd obviously found a deep connection with you. There might be a reason he's trying to reach out to you. Remember, you're the one he chose to trust with the secret of the gold."

"Joseph," Maddie asked, "is there a way to know? To find out if they are really just dreams, or if there is something more spiritual going on?"

Joseph nodded very slowly, a solemn look on his face. "I agree with Emmett that Askuwheteau chose Billy Mac—a bond was made. Perhaps his spirit remains a guardian to Billy Mac."

"Is there a way?" Maddie repeated her question.

"There is a way," Joseph answered, still solemn and apprehensive. "One cannot be assured of making the connection. But, if one is pure of heart, sincere in their desire to connect with their guardian, and willing to undertake the trials, there is a way to try."

"Is it dangerous?" Emmett asked.

Joseph thought for a moment. "It is not dangerous. But it is an arduous journey." His smiled returned. "It can be grueling and difficult, but I would be happy to assist with the effort."

Joseph, Maddie, and Emmett all turned to Billy Mac and waited.

Billy Mac hung his head. A minute passed. He took a deep breath, exhaled, then looked up at his three friends. "Okay," he said and forced a not very convincing grin. "I'll try. How do we do it?"

Joseph thought for a minute and then looked at his friends. "There is preparation I need to do," he said. "Come out to the cabin early next Saturday morning. I will clear it with father— he can cover the shop that day. I will have everything ready. We can talk through it in more detail and begin if Billy Mac still chooses to do so. But, be aware—the ritual and process may take days. One never knows how soon—or even if—their guardian will show themselves. All we can do is try."

Billy Mac gulped, and then held his hand out, palm down. The others stacked their hands on top of his, looked at each other, and nodded.

The sky was clouded over. No stars, no moon. No breeze. Just a hot, sticky night that made it hard to sleep. The crickets were loud. Cicadas and tree frogs were starting to come out, their drones and croaking played against each other.

"Emmo," Billy Mac asked, "what's it like working down at the dam?"

"Pretty interesting, but pretty demanding," Emmett replied from his cot. "A lot of hard work."

"Hmmm," was all Billy Mac replied.

"Something bothering you, Mackie?"

"Maybe a little."

"Want to talk about it?"

Billy Mac lay in silence for a minute.

"Remember last summer when we talked about your father and my mother, wonderin' if they looked down on us, watched over us?"

"Yeah," Emmett answered.

"Remember what you said?"

"Yeah," Emmett answered again. "I said I hoped maybe they did. That it made me feel good to think that maybe they did."

"Yeah," Billy Mac said. "Me, too."

"So?"

"So, I still do. But I guess maybe in the back of my mind I'm not sure I ever really believed it, maybe just hoped because it made me feel good."

"And?"

Billy Mac rolled onto his side, facing the dark silhouette of Emmett on his cot.

"I'm a little wigged out thinking that maybe spirits might be real—and that I'm going to try to see one face-to-face and talk to one."

"Are you afraid?" Emmett asked. "It's okay if you are—anyone might be. Me, too."

Billy Mac rolled back over and looked up into the cloudy night.

"Not really afraid," he said. "Just trying to come to grips that maybe something's real. Before it was okay not knowing. Just different now that it might be real."

"It might be, or it might not be," Emmett said. "It might just be tribal lore, a part of their tradition."

"Yeah. Night, Emmo."

"Night, Mackie."

Billy Mac closed his eyes. *I'm gonna try, Askuwheteau,* he thought. *I promise I'll try.*

Chapter 7

Ahote had been walking the tracks most of the day. He paused to get his bearings. Monticello—his hometown—was only about ten miles away. He remembered a road that crossed the tracks about a mile ahead. He'd camp close to it. It would be dark soon. There was just enough food left in his bindle sack for one more night. In the morning he could probably hitch a ride on a wagon to get in close to town. Tonight, he'd think through his story of who he was going to be—the identity he wanted to assume—and brush up on his looks.

In the dusk he saw the road crossing ahead, then he smelled the smoke. Someone was camping nearby. Probably hobos. If he played his cards right, he could probably horn in on them— the Code allowed it. Hopefully, it wasn't any rail riders he'd known who would make him push on.

He neared the road crossing, followed the smell of the smoke, and smiled. Bacon. He loved bacon and the taste of bread mopped in the frying pan grease. Maybe they have some beans, too.

He stepped onto the gravel road that crossed the tracks and cautiously worked his way into the trees. He wanted to be able to see them and check them out for a few minutes before he approached their camp.

He slipped from tree to tree, careful not to step on any sticks. He peered carefully through the thicket and was surprised by what he saw. A covered wagon with a horse tethered nearby. Then he heard a voice offer the end of a prayer he'd known well since he was a child.

"...may our grief be lifted, our hearts be open, our stomach be full, our bones be braced, and our will be calmed. It is spoken, it is beautiful."

Ahote was shocked. *One of The People? Here?*

He moved around the tree for a better look. The man bent over and poked at the contents in the frying pan propped on the rocks off to one side of the small fire.

Older than me, Ahote thought. *Nice clothes.* He looked a little closer. *Wagon in good shape. Horse well groomed. Clean, well-kept campsite. I should be able to do well here if I play it right.*

Ahote stepped from the trees a short way and then stopped. "Aya akime," he called.

The man at the fire stood up and turned, a surprised look on his face. "Aya niihka," he slowly returned the formal salutation.

"Neehahki?" Ahote asked with a smile as he went full bore into the act and pretense of a friend.

The man studied him for a moment. Ahote's false charm disarmed the man and he answered, "Nahatwi. It is well. Please join me at my fire."

"Mihsi neewe," Ahote called his thanks as he walked into the campsite. "I heard and smelled your fire—and your supper." Ahote smiled and nodded at the frying pan, the bacon just about ready to eat.

"You are just in time," the man warmed to Ahote and returned the smile. "There is enough for two. Please be seated and I will prepare for us both." He waved to a log next to the fire.

"My name is Taregan," the man called over his shoulder as he retrieved two tin plate pans from the sideboard of his wagon. He put bread onto both plates, walked to the fire, put bacon on each plate, and handed one to Ahote.

Ahote had to think fast. There was no way he'd offer his real name to this person, or any other. After last summer, it was a certainty his name had been circulated to state authorities and to the members of the various Indian nations.

"I am Ahanu," Ahote chuckled, playing the role as he lied to the man.

Taregan smiled. "He-who-laughs? It is a name that seems to fit you well." Then he asked, "How is it a myaamia came to find my little campsite?"

Ahote told a partial truth—he had been out west but was slowly working his way back home, back to Monticello, where he had been born and raised. His elderly father—whom he loved and greatly missed—still lived there. He wanted to return home, to spend whatever time his father had left together with him.

"But, what about you, Taregan?" Ahote asked. "I was just as surprised by you as you were of me."

"I have been sent by the elders of our Nation," Taregan explained. "I travel to Monticello to seek council with the sheriff, some kwiiw and ahkweehs."

Ahote stiffened with alarm but quickly composed himself.

"Some young men and a young woman," he smiled and repeated after Taregan. "I'm sure you will be of great help to them, in whatever course of matter they seek the Nation's council." Ahote needed to coax information out of this man.

"I hope, but I am not sure." Taregan furrowed his eyebrows in thought. "It is most mysterious. One of the young people is of the Nation. The others are not. Their letter to the elders requested an urgent visit by a representative of the Nation in a matter that they feel is of great interest to us. I am most curious. The letter implied no further information can be shared until a visit can take place and to keep their request in the strictest of confidence."

Realizing his mistake, Taregan added, "I suppose I should not even be discussing it with you."

The darkness in Ahote rose and he fought to repress it. *They found it,* he thought. *They found the gold. They must have.*

Ahote took another look at Taregan, quickly measured him up, and realized he'd found the identity he was going to assume when he went to town tomorrow. *It would be easy,* he thought. *We're the same size. I won't even have to dye my hair—most members of the Nation have similar features. Of those four kids, only one of them saw him for a brief moment, and it was at night in the middle of a raging thunderstorm while they struggled with each other. And, no problem with the sheriff. They had not seen each other in years.*

Ahote reverted to his role-playing. "No concern," he chuckled. "In fact, I am a close friend of the sheriff. We grew up together. If you'll permit me to accompany you to town in the morning, I would be pleased to make introductions."

"Teepaatamaani." Taregan expressed his thanks with relief. "I would be indebted. Now, while the wagon has only the room for one to sleep, I will bring you some blankets to bed down by the fire. It looks to be a clear, warm night."

"It is I who am indebted." Ahote bowed slightly.

He stood up as Taregan turned and walked to the back of the wagon. *Indebted more than you know,* he thought with a sneer. He quietly followed the older man.

Taregan reached inside the back of the wagon to lift some blankets out, thought he heard a sound behind him, and started to turn, but wasn't fast enough. From behind, Ahote grabbed his head, and with a quick twist Taregan floated into darkness.

Chapter 8

Billy Mac, Emmett, and Maddie—the latter holding hands—walked up the grassy lane. Boomer followed behind, back and forth from one side of the lane to the other, sniffing along the edges where the shorter grass met the higher scrub that outlined the lane.

Billy Mac, as usual, carried his backpack. It included his sketchpad, charcoal, and pencils. He had a natural artistic ability. It also carried a few changes of clothes. No telling how long he'd be at Joseph's cabin.

The lane was familiar to all of them. They'd made the trip multiple times to visit Askuwheteau when he lived here along the bluffs. Sycamore and cottonwood trees lined it on both sides—the shade was nice.

After Askuwheteau's death, the county found a will he had drawn up in which he left the cabin and its belongings to Joseph's family. They'd been so kind to him for so many years, looking in on him from time to time. Joseph's father and mother lived in town with Joseph's younger siblings. So, Joseph and Henry, the family horse, moved out to the cabin last fall and Joseph built a snug shelter along one side of the cabin for Henry.

The lane was even more familiar to Billy Mac than the others at this point—he'd seen it recently in the dreams he'd had in which he'd heard Askuwheteau calling to him. Those dreams had led to their visit to Joseph and the cabin today.

They rounded the bend that opened up to the cabin, which sat on the bluffs of the river. A cliff rose behind it and along one side, protecting it from wind and weather from the north and east. Billy Mac had always liked the peaceful setting here. The cicadas droned with their eee-eee-eee-AH-AH-AH-AH cadence that rose and fell. The disk-shaped leaves of the cottonwoods flicked in the breeze and made the sound of swift water flowing in a steam.

Joseph, sitting in the shade of the porch on a bench beside the front door, waved as they rounded the bend. Billy Mac sat down beside him as Emmett and Maddie sat together on a bench on the other side of the doorway. Boomer plopped down on the porch in the shade at their feet.

"Pretty day, Joseph," Maddie said as she scratched Boomer's head.

"Sure is," Joseph answered. He turned and looked at Billy Mac. "Still want to go through with this?"

"I do," Billy Mac sighed. "I think it's the right thing to do."

"It doesn't always work," Joseph reminded him. "And, you have to sincerely really want to do it—deep down inside to the core of your being—or it doesn't stand a chance of happening."

"I know," Billy Mac nodded. "I really want to do it. Honest."

"I've done some homework at the library, Joseph," Emmett said. "From what I found, a vision quest is usually sought by a young member of the tribe trying to connect with a guardian spirit—most of the time, an animal. It can help define that person and give them insight as to the direction their life should take. And, it usually requires the help of a shaman or medicine man to start the ritual and then to help interpret the vision."

"Good job, Emmett," Joseph said. "That's correct."

Jeff Darnell

"It usually starts with a sweat lodge, and then the person moves out into nature to fast and seek the vision, right?" Emmett asked.

"Correct, again," Joseph said.

"But, Joseph," Maddie began, "how do we do this without a medicine man and a sweat lodge to start in?"

"I think we have an advantage," Joseph explained. "Rather than us initiating a connection, I believe we already have a guardian spirit seeking to make a connection from the other side. So, I believe it is possible our task may be easier because of that. The role of a medicine man can sometimes be ceremonial, so I believe we may proceed without that benefit. And, it is easy to create somewhat of a sweat lodge in the cabin—we start a fire and make it hot in there. I have one prepared in the hearth already. This will be necessary as sweating purifies our bodies. Fasting will further purify the body, and also the mind, as a sign to the spirits that the person attempting the vision quest is worthy. Although Billy Mac will fast, with the help of Father I have prepared an herbal tea that will help Billy Mac relax, focus, and meditate."

88

"What about going into the wild by himself to seek the vision after the sweat?" Emmett asked.

"I don't think it is needed," Joseph further explained. "It would be necessary if Billy Mac were seeking a vision to connect with an animal guardian. But we aren't doing that. We simply want his body and mind to be receptive to the spirit we believe has been reaching out to him. We may be able to accomplish that by the sweat and fasting regimen, along with proper meditation. And, we may have an advantage making those efforts here—at the cabin Askuwheteau lived in, and died in."

Everyone nodded in agreement and sat in silence for a few minutes.

"Joseph," Billy Mac finally asked, "what can I expect?"

"Hard to say," Joseph shrugged. "The sweat will only last for about three hours and will tire you out a little. You'll know when it's time to stop. At that point we'll extinguish the fire, and I'll then leave you alone inside the cabin to fast and meditate. I'll always be right here, outside the door. Depending on how long you fast after the sweat, you may or may not experience discomfort. If the fast lasts long—a day or two—

your hunger will go away. You may have headaches and dizziness that will then give way to an anxious, jittery feeling and you may not be able to sleep. During it all, meditation will come easier to you as time goes by."

"If I have the vision, will it happen when I'm asleep—in a dream—or when I'm awake?" Billy Mac asked.

"Those having reported success of their vision quests have reported both," Joseph said. "And, sometimes it happens when you're awake, but with your eyes closed. There's no way to know from person to person how their vision quest will unfold. Mine happened one way; Father's happened another."

"Okay," Billy Mac said after a few moments and stood up. "I'm ready."

The others stood up and came together. Emmett held his hand out, palm down. The others all laid theirs on top. "Good luck, Mackie," Emmett said and nodded at him. He looked a little concerned.

"Boomer and I will check on you both," Maddie said. "Gramps will be happy to drive me over each day."

"I'll be working at the dam each day," Emmett said, "but will get out if I can."

"We'll be fine," Joseph assured them. "I have plenty of provisions. I know Father will be stopping by, as well. Billy Mac is in good hands."

Maddie leaned forward and hugged Billy Mac. She stepped back and Billy Mac, somewhat embarrassed, gave Maddie and Emmett an awkward smile. "Thanks" was all he could think to say, and then he turned and walked into the cabin.

Joseph followed and closed the door behind them.

Chapter 9

It had been a nice morning, sunny and pleasant. Ahote had made breakfast over the fire and then went to the creek to wash up—he had to be presentable when he showed up at the sheriff's office. He'd changed into the best suit of clothes he'd found in the wagon and then loaded up everything from the campsite. Ahote stepped up into the wagon, released the hand brake, and then snapped the reins and the horse started with a jolt.

He smiled to himself—things couldn't be better. After disposing of Taregan's body the night before he'd gone through everything in the wagon. The clothes fit him perfectly. He'd found some money—not a lot, but enough to see him through this charade. There were plenty of provisions for him and the horse—enough for a couple weeks if he stretched it. He'd also found the letter Joseph and the sheriff had sent to the Miami council of elders, and a return letter of introduction from the elders for Taregan to present to the sheriff when he reached Monticello. Then, he'd bedded down in the wagon and slept better than he had for a long time. What he had done—and what he was about to do—didn't bother him in the slightest.

He'd found a mirror and scissors in the wagon, so he'd cut his hair to fashion it after Taregan, and then practiced some of Taregan's mannerisms and expressions. He'd even surprised himself—the resemblance was striking. This was going to be a breeze. He sneered and scoffed at the thought of Taregan. Tough luck, old man.

Ahote drove the wagon onto the road toward town and thought about his good fortune. True—he could take the horse and wagon, with everything in it, and head out of state. No one would miss Taregan for a few weeks. By the time they did, he'd be long gone. He could live pretty well for a while with what he had. But he could live better once he played the role and got his hands on the gold those kids found. The mere thought of them dredged up the hate and anger he'd been chewing on over the past year. If something unfortunate happened to them while he worked his way to the gold, so much the better.

By midday he approached the outskirts of town. Ahote reached into his shirt pocket, pulled out the fake spectacles, and put them on. *Here we go,* he thought.

An hour later he was done and climbing back onto the bench of the wagon. He released the hand brake, snapped the reins, and was on his way. *My God, how easy that was!* It was all he could do not to bust out laughing. The sheriff never suspected anything. Why would he? He'd had the letter of introduction and he'd played the role perfectly. He was the well-spoken, well-dressed, honorable elder, concerned only with assisting the sheriff and citizens of their fine community in any way he could. What a crock.

The sheriff had told him Askuwheteau was dead. Ahote smiled. That made things even better. Askuwheteau—his estranged father—was the only concern he'd had. He would have been the only one that could have exposed Ahote's ruse. He felt no sorrow or remorse. Why should he? The old man had meant nothing to him. Hadn't his father always refused to share the secret of the gold with him? His death only made Ahote's farse easier.

The sheriff had suggested Ahote stay in the hotel, but Ahote refused. It would be too easy for others to see him come and go.

He wouldn't be able to sneak around very easily. So, he'd played the role and told the sheriff that as a humble elder of the Miami nation, he liked to live close to mother earth. He would make a simple camp on the outskirts of town. The sheriff suggested he camp on the far edge of the park, alongside the river. This suited Ahote perfectly.

The sheriff had explained that although he wasn't able to offer any details as to the purpose of the letter to the elder council, he would gather Billy Mac, Emmett, Joseph, and Maddie as soon as possible, and bring them to Ahote's camp. They could discuss everything then. *Fine,* he thought. This suited him perfectly.

Now that he was far enough away from the town square and the sheriff's office, he laughed out loud.

Chapter 10

Billy Mac walked into the one-room cabin and saw Joseph had made a pallet for him in the middle of the floor facing the fireplace. There were a few blankets on top of the wood floor and a few more folded and stacked for him to lean back on. Billy Mac sat on the pallet a little unsure of himself, not quite sure what to do.

Joseph lit the fire he had already built in the hearth. He had lined the inside with large stones to help radiate the heat. Then he came and sat down on the floor opposite Billy Mac.

"What'll I do?" Billy Mac asked him.

"Nothing," Joseph shrugged. "Whatever you want to do or whatever you feel like doing. Once it gets heated up in here, you'll likely want to undress some because you'll start to sweat. I'll fix your tea. It may help you relax, and it may help you kind of daydream. Or, it may not. You'll just have to see. The goal is to spend time in the sweat. I'll do the sweat with you. We'll know when it's time to stop. I'll then leave you inside the cabin by yourself to continue with your fast and mediation. I'll leave some wood next to the hearth with some resin incense. Keep some coals going and add incense to the top of one of the heat stones every now and then. It will help you focus as you meditate. In the meantime, do whatever you'd like. I'll fix your tea now."

Billy Mac looked around the cabin. Simple, nice, and neat. It looked exactly as it did when Askuwheteau had lived here. The cot in the corner, blankets folded neatly on it. A Franklin stove and sink with a well pump on one wall, a window above the sink. The hearth on the opposite wall. The back door with the pegs above it on which rested the shotgun that had belonged to Askuwheteau. Joseph had moved the table and chairs from the center of the room off to one side to make room for Billy Mac's pallet.

Billy Mac opened his backpack and took out his sketchpad and a few pencils. He flipped though it and studied the last few sketches he'd made. They were from his dreams of walking down the grassy lane in the mist toward the cabin. He flipped to a blank page, studied the room, glanced at Joseph fixing tea on the stove, and started sketching.

Thirty minutes later the cabin began to heat up. Billy Mac stowed his sketchpad and pencils into the backpack and sipped the tea Joseph had brought him. It tasted of mint. He took off his shirt, undershirt, shoes, and socks. He was definitely sweating. He glanced over at the cot—Joseph was sitting with his back straight, cross-legged with hands in his lap. He was bare to the waist, too. His eyes were closed, and he looked so peaceful taking slow, steady breaths.

Billy Mac copied Joseph's pose and closed his eyes. The tea was having its effect and it seemed to open the passages in his head. He could breathe easy, deeper, almost without effort. He felt relaxed and a little spacey. Or, maybe it was the heat of the sweat. *Maybe a little of both*, he thought. He concentrated into a rhythmic, comfortable deep breathing pattern. He couldn't remember a time when he'd ever felt more peaceful and relaxed.

He kept his eyes closed and his mind wandered, unaware of how much time passed. When he came back to awareness a time or two, he fought the impulse to open his eyes. He let the awareness fade and his mind wandered again.

Something was different. The heat was gone. Billy Mac was surprised at how much effort it took to open his eyes. He blinked a few times and took a deep breath. The fire had gone out, only some glowing embers left. And, it was mostly dark. Faint light from a starry sky came through the two windows. He moved to put his undershirt and shirt back on. Then his shoes and socks. Although his skin crinkled from the dried, salty sweat, he surprisingly felt cleansed.

How much time had passed? No telling. Joseph was gone. He'd said he'd leave after the sweat. Next to Billy Mac on the floor was another cup of tea—now cold—and a glass of water. He took a long drink of each, crawled to the fireplace, put a split log on the coals to keep them going, took some incense resin from the bowl, and put it on one of the hot rocks lining the inside of the hearth. A small trail of smoke circled into the cabin—the smell of fresh pine trees.

Billy Mac crawled back to his pallet, leaned against the stack of blankets into a comfortable position, and closed his eyes, aware of the growling hunger in his stomach. *Hope Joseph's right,* he thought. *I hope these hunger pangs pass soon.* His stomach growled even louder.

Feeling a little fatigued from the sweat and lack of food, Billy Mac closed his eyes. The tea helped him relax and the pine incense did the trick—it did give him something to focus on. In that realm between awake and asleep, between reality and dream, Billy Mac smelled the incense. He fashioned himself in the midst of a pine forest and drew himself into it.

Strange, the colors, he thought. *Stunningly vivid. I thought all pine trees were green. Huh! Guess not. The purple ones are neat. Emmett would like those. He always did like the color purple. Maddie would like the pink ones. They look like cotton candy. Why is the sky yellow? Huh! Look at that funny little fox with the white spot on his forehead. What a remarkable place.*

Billy Mac walked through the painted forest with an immense feeling of joy and peace. Time passed effortlessly. It could have been hours or days.

A noise brought him back to reality. He opened a lazy eye to see Joseph put more tea and water on the floor beside him, another small piece of wood on the embers in the hearth, and more incense on the heat stone, and then quietly leave the cabin. Daylight streamed through the windows.

Billy Mac sat up straight, the feeling of joy and peace still with him. He sipped the fresh tea and felt totally refreshed with a rush of energy. His hunger pangs were gone, and his senses quickened. Without moving he was somehow aware of everything inside the cabin and out, as if an inner eye allowed him to see and know. He crossed his legs, closed his eyes, and focused on that inner eye, more awake and more aware than he'd ever been before.

Time didn't exist. Billy Mac's sense of peace and sense of self pervaded deep into his being just as his energy and awareness transcended outward. He could feel those forces radiate from him in a shower of color. He opened his eyes and saw the world differently, in a soft, milky haze. A rainbow of colors flowed from him and enveloped him. Everything shone through the site of the inner eye he had found. And, it brought a deeper peace, still. Time didn't exist.

Billy Mac knew he was there, even before he heard him. He wasn't startled, the serenity in him complete. He opened his eyes and as before, everything glowed with its own aura, including Askuwheteau sitting across from him. To the left of him sat a red fox with a white spot on its forehead, its green eyes watching Billy Mac intently.

"Be-zone, neekanhuh," Askuwheteau said.

"Be-zone, akotha," Billy Mac answered, using the respectful word Joseph had taught him to address an elder. "I had hoped you would come."

"I have tried before but could not reach thee."

"I know," Billy Mac said. "I am sorry. I did not know how." He nodded at the fox. "Who is this with you?"

"This paapankamw is my guardian spirit," Askuwheteau said. "He I found as a kwiiwihs when I sought my vision quest. He watched over me during my lifetime—now he will watch over you during yours. You will know him by his mark." Askuwheteau pointed to the white spot on the fox's forehead.

"But why, akotha?"

"The paapankamw is cunning and wise," Askuwheteau said. "He is aware but stays well hidden. He sees through the falseness of those who would harm him. He is clever to escape when danger abounds. So must you be. I sense a darkness—a presence of one who would harm thee and thy friends. The paapankamw will help you. Look to him for guidance."

Billy Mac looked at the fox and nodded. "I will," he said. "But, of what danger do you speak?"

"It is not clear. You must use your new vision and beware."

"Is this why you sought me?" Billy Mac asked. "I thought perhaps there was more. You once tried to tell me where to find that which was hidden many years ago, that which was watched over by those of The People who had taken vows. Your father was one such."

"Yes," Askuwheteau answered. "This is true. 'Twas part of my journey to seek thee." He turned to his right. "Can you see no other here, to my side?"

"No," Billy Mac answered. "I see no other."

"My father is here with me, he who watched over that which is hidden. It was he who moved it for safety. Our purpose was to let thee know to look for that which he left behind, for those after him to know the place. Seek thee his message. It will guide thee."

"But, akotha, we found the cave where it had been hidden. There was no message. Nothing to tell us to look elsewhere. No clue or map. There must be a mistake. Can you tell me more?"

"Our visit ends, neekanhuh. Take guidance from paapankamw." He nodded at the fox. "Beware the untruths of darkness and seek the message left thee by him who came before."

"Wait—I don't understand," Billy Mac pleaded. "Wait, akotha!"

"Goodbye, neekanhuh. Peace be with thee."

Then, he and the fox were gone.

Chapter 11

It was the following Saturday morning. Billy Mac, Joseph, Emmett, and Maddie sat on the benches in the shade under the sycamore tree outside the blacksmith shop.

"And, then it was over," Billy Mac finished telling the others about the vision. "I sat there, a little confused. I closed my eyes to concentrate, to think it all through. I wanted to make sure I'd remember everything. When I opened my eyes, everything was back to normal. Nothing was glowing anymore. Everything was just as if nothing had happened. And, I was exhausted. Totally drained."

"Joseph, could you hear anything?" Maddie asked.

"Not clearly," he answered. "From my bench outside the door, I could hear that Billy Mac was talking, but I couldn't make out his words. And, I didn't hear anything from anyone else. But, that's not unusual. Askuwheteau's words were for Billy Mac only. No one else other than Billy Mac could have seen or heard Askuwheteau, even if they had been in the room at the same time."

"And then?" Emmett asked.

"And then I got up, walked outside, and sat down next to Joseph," Billy Mac said.

"You should have seen him," Joseph chuckled. "He just looked horrible!"

"You would, too, if you hadn't eaten or really slept for two and a half days," Billy Mac smiled.

"Nothing that a good meal and some sleep didn't fix," Joseph added.

"You did it, Mackie—you really did it!" Emmett slapped him on the back. "Good man!"

"So, the mystery continues, though," Maddie said.

"Right. Let's talk about how we proceed," Joseph suggested.

"I think we keep Mackie's vision with Askuwheteau to ourselves for now," Emmett said. "Not tell anyone else about it, except the sheriff. I'm sure Billy Mac would like to tell his pa about it."

"But what else do we do for now?" Joseph repeated.

"Well, Pa wants us to go with him to meet that elder sent by the Miami council," Billy Mac said. "I told him we'd meet him at his office in a little while, okay?"

"Sure, Mackie," Emmett said.

"I can go," Maddie said, tilting her head and brushing her bangs off to the side. "Boomer and I are staying in town a few days with Aunt Charlotte."

"I cannot," Joseph said. "I have much work to do." He stood up and tied his leather apron back on. "But, keep me posted if you learn anything from him."

They all agreed, and then Billy Mac, Emmett, and Maddie walked down to the street and turned toward the sheriff's office.

Billy Mac and Emmett lay in their cots on Billy Mac's back porch. It was another sticky night with not much of a breeze. It always seemed to get still once the sun set. The heat really brought out the crickets, cicadas, and tree frogs. They took turns with their chirping, droning, and croaking. One group would fade away for a bit, and the others would pick up. Amazing how loud nighttime could be sometimes.

"How was supper?" Billy Mac asked Emmett. He'd just gotten to Billy Mac's house.

Emmett had had supper with Maddie at her Aunt Charlotte's house in town. Emmett and Maddie both tried to get Billy Mac to join them, too, but he increasingly felt in the way. Once again, he'd made excuses and opted out.

"Good," Emmett said. "You sure missed out. Miss Charlotte's a great cook, and a nice lady."

"Anything new?"

"A lot of talk about Maddie's cousin, Becky, that will be here before long. She'll be staying and going to school here. Maddie's pretty excited about it. She's our age. Made me promise we'd make her feel welcomed."

"Humph," Billy Mac grunted.

"I promised her, Mackie. You have to help."

"Yeah, sure. Okay," Billy Mac promised. "What'd you think about Taregan today? I kinda had a funny feeling about him. Something about him give me the creeps."

"Seemed like a nice enough guy. Boomer sure didn't take to him, either, did he?" Emmett chuckled. "I've never seen him act that way with anyone. Anyway, I don't know how much help he'll be since he didn't know anything about the legend of Tecumseh's missing gold."

"But he promised to check with his council back at their reservation. Maybe someone there will have something. Anything."

"Maybe. He sure is anxious to see that gold bar down at the jailhouse. Remember, we have to meet him and your pa there tomorrow at lunchtime," Emmett said.

"Right," Billy Mac said. "We'll get up and eat, get the eggs from the henhouse and take them to take to market, and then go down to the jailhouse."

"Not me, Mackie. I promised Ma I'd meet her at The Strand real early. She got that new projector in. We're going to start showing movies instead of just having the normal circuit of people and groups coming through. I gotta start working on figuring it out and setting it up. It'll be nice to have picture shows here in town. People won't have to go all the way to Lafayette anymore. And, get this—Ma says talkies are coming.

Can you imagine? Moving pictures that have sound? Sure is gonna be something!"

"Sure will!" Billy Mac agreed. "Talkies. How funny!"

"Anyway, after we're done at the jailhouse I need to go down to the worksite at the dam. You should come with me."

"On a Sunday afternoon? How come?"

"There's a spot, a little gap in the bluff wall that's real shady. There are trees all around it. Me and the other workers go there for our lunch breaks. We found a skeleton of a person and some animals—maybe dogs. Pretty good size ones. Purdue is sending over some people from their university to check them out. They're coming this afternoon. I want to be there."

"Skeletons? And, you want to be there? For what?"

"You know me, Mackie. Always interested in learning new things. As Principal Skinner would say, 'Endeavor always to expand one's capacity.'"

"You and Skinner sure are a pair. That's something I've learned!" Billy Mac laughed.

"But besides that, the work down at the dam is incredible," Emmett said. "It's going to be fifty-eight feet high. The turbines in it that will make electricity for town here are massive. You should come with me and check it all out. It actually has me thinking that maybe I'll study to be an engineer. Purdue is a really good university. They've had an engineering department for forty or fifty years. Maybe I could study there and be a mechanical engineer. I could build things."

"Instead of being a writer?" Billy Mac asked. "I thought you always wanted to be a writer. You always loved reading so much. You even got me to read the Sherlock Holmes stories, which I have to admit were pretty good. The writing you've done is pretty good. Even Ms. Lee thinks so."

"I can always write. I always will. I do love it. But there's so much going on. The last *Popular Mechanics* I got had an article about a guy in Massachusetts named Goddard who just shot off a liquid-fuel rocket. That's nuts! A rocket! Someday people will go to the moon! There's going to be tons of stuff for mechanical engineers to work on."

"You're dreamin', Emmo," Billy Mac said, a little sleepy. "No way a person is ever goin' to the moon."

"You wait, Mackie. They will. But anyway, you should go down to the dam with me tomorrow."

"Skeletons, huh?"

"Yeah. Skeletons."

"Okay. I'll go with you."

"Good man!" Emmett said and rolled over on his cot. "Night, Mackie."

"Night, Emmo."

Chapter 12

Ahote finished his breakfast and spread the coals of the fire. He walked down to the edge of the river to wash himself, his tin plate, fork, and knife. He straightened up the wagon and made the campsite neat—he had to keep up appearances. Then he changed into clean clothes, put his fake glasses into his shirt pocket, fed the horse, and started the walk into town.

He thought through everything from the day before when the sheriff and some of the kids came to his camp for introductions. The dog bothered him. It was obvious it sensed something it didn't like. Could it have remembered him from a year ago? Is that possible? If it became a problem, he'd have to do something about it. No way he was going to let a stupid mutt derail his shot at something this big.

And, it was something big. The fact that the kids had found a bar of gold proved that. He'd never known if the legend and stories were real or not. But here it was. They found gold. The thought of it quickened his pulse and made his stomach turn over a few times. *Real gold! There has to be more—it just has to be found. That tall boy seemed pretty smart,* Ahote thought. *Well, I can be smart, too. Just play the role, find reasons to stick around and give the appearance of trying to be helpful. Let the kids keep playing detective, keep a close eye on them, then move in when the mystery's solved. And, maybe even the score with that short kid, too.* He caused a lot of grief last year. The thought of it made him smile.

When Billy Mac got up, Emmett was long gone. He washed, dressed, and did the normal morning routines—checked the ice block, the wood box, the kerosene in the lanterns and trimmed the wicks. He made the rounds through the two chicken houses and then cleaned and boxed up the eggs. He picked up the stack of egg cartons and headed toward town, letting the screen door bang close behind him.

He walked into the jailhouse and everyone was there—Emmett, Maddie without Boomer, Joseph, his father, and Ahote posing as Taregan.

"Morning," he said, nodding at everyone. "Where's Boomer, Maddie?"

"I thought it would be best if I left him at Aunt Charlotte's," she said, brushing her bangs out of her eyes.

"Thank you." Ahote's Taregan character was all smiles. "That's very kind of you. Sometimes dogs just don't like me. I'm more of a cat person." He smiled again.

"Well," the sheriff began and sat down at his desk, "let's get started." He took the key ring off his belt, selected the proper one, fitted it into the lock of one of the desk drawers, turned it, pulled open the drawer, took out an object wrapped in a cloth, and set it on his desk. "I think this is what you've come to see." He opened the cloth and everyone gathered around to look at the gold bar.

Ahote's stomach turned over again. "Oh, my," he said breathlessly. "May I hold it?"

"Sure," the sheriff answered. "Help yourself."

Ahote stepped forward and picked it up, weighing it up and down in his hand. Billy Mac watched his face carefully. *What is it about him?* he wondered. *There's something about him that's just not right.*

For some reason, Billy Mac looked past the group. His focus moved to a framed picture on the far wall. It had always been there—a print of an old nineteenth century English fox hunt. The red fox ran in the foreground, while multiple hounds scurried in hot pursuit followed by English nobility in their iconic gear on their horses. He walked over to look at it more closely, and the conversation of the others faded into the background.

He'd never really paid attention to the print before; he was just aware that it had always been there. He looked at the fox, squinted for a closer look, and caught his breath. It had a small white spot on its forehead. Unbelievable.

Billy Mac remembered Askuwheteau's words. *This paapankamw is my guardian spirit. He watched over me during my lifetime—now he will watch over you during yours. You will know him by his mark. The paapankamw is cunning and wise. He is aware but stays well hidden. He sees through the falseness of those who would harm him. He is clever to escape when danger abounds. So must you be. Take guidance from the paapankamw. Beware the untruths of darkness.*

Billy Mac closed his eyes and found the inner eye that had come to him during his vision quest. He slowly opened his eyes and then turned to look at the others as they talked among themselves. They all emitted color, a type of glow—it was amazing! His father, Emmett, Maddie, and Joseph were all surrounded with brilliant colors that radiated from them. Deep red, orange, yellow, green—even a bright white.

But the person known as Taregan didn't. He was enveloped in a layer of black that clung to him. *Amazing!* Billy Mac thought.

His father startled him back to the present. "Billy Mac. Are you listening to me?"

Billy Mac blinked a few times and everything was back to normal. The colors were gone. He forced a lopsided smile. "Sorry, Pa. What were you saying?"

"I asked if there was anything else you wanted to share with Taregan." He was obviously referring to Billy Mac's vision quest with Askuwheteau, asking if he wanted to share the information with Taregan.

"Uhm. No, Pa. Nothing I can think of." He forced another smile.

"Okay," the sheriff said, giving Billy Mac a quizzical look. "I guess that's it for now then."

"Thank you, Sheriff," Ahote's Taregan character said, shaking his hand and nodding to the others. "As I said, I await word back from our council of elders. I will let you all know when I have done so. In the meantime, please call upon me if I may be of service."

"You know, Taregan," the sheriff said. "I think I will reach out to the Shawnee council in Oklahoma. Since Tecumseh was a member of one of their tribes...which one was it?" He looked around at everyone.

"Kispoko," Emmett said. "He was born into the Kispoko tribe, along the Scioto River near present-day Chillicothe, Ohio."

"Right. Since he was a member of the Shawnee Kispoko tribe, they might know something of this mystery."

Ahote thought fast. "No need, Sheriff," he said with a smile. "Perhaps that is another way I may be of service. One of our elders has very close ties with the Shawnee council. I will ask him to reach out on your behalf."

"That would be most helpful," the sheriff replied, and they shook hands again. "Many thanks."

Ahote made his way back to his camp on the far side of the city park. He took his glasses off, put them in his pocket, and scowled, his face twisted with rage. He had been unnerved by the way Billy Mac looked at him. *What is it with that kid?* he wondered. *Always a problem. Just another reason for him to get his due at some point. If that dog becomes a problem, I'll take care of it. If that kid becomes a problem, well, that can be taken care of, too.* He scowled, again.

Chapter 13

They had walked Maddie back to her Aunt Charlotte's house. She and Emmett sat on the porch swing, Boomer at their feet. Joseph and Billy Mac sat on the porch steps.

"Anyone else think that was weird?" Billy Mac asked, kicking at the ground with the toe of his shoe.

"Nothing I can think of, Mackie," Emmett answered.

"No, not really," Maddie said.

"Nor I," Joseph said. "How come?"

Billy Mac turned to look at his friends. "Remember in my vision at one point I opened my eyes and everything was kind of hazy? It was like I was looking through some kind of filmy window. And, these colors poured out of me and surrounded me. It was like I had a new way of looking at things, a way to see more than I could see before. I don't know how to put it."

Billy Mac looked at the ground and shook his head. "I'm not sure I can explain it."

"It's a gift," Joseph said. "You have a new gift that many people wish they had."

"What do you mean, Joseph?" Maddie asked.

"I have heard medicine men speak of it. I believe as Billy Mac learns how to channel this new vision, he will learn how to interpret and use it to his benefit, and to the benefit of others."

"But what is it?" Maddie asked.

"I believe I know what Joseph's talking about," Emmett said. "I've read about it before."

"And?" Billy Mac asked.

"Some people believe living things, even plants, emit an energy field," Emmett said. "Sometimes that energy field gives off colors. The color of a person's energy field can be an indication as to the wellness of their physical being as well as their spiritual being. Some people have the ability to see the colors of that energy field. Is that accurate, Joseph?"

"Yes, very accurate," Joseph nodded.

"It's not something unique to Native Americans," Emmett said. "It's something that some people all around the world have experienced for thousands of years."

"What does that have to do with today?" Maddie asked.

"Remember Askuwheteau said that fox would look after me, and to use him for guidance?" Billy Mac said. "Well, while you all were talking with Pa and Taregan, I noticed something. In that picture on the wall in the jailhouse, there's a fox that looks just like the one in my vision."

"But a fox is a fox, isn't it?" Maddie asked. "And, how long has that picture been hanging there?"

"For as long as I can remember," Emmett said.

"Me, too," Billy Mac answered. "But, that fox in my vision, he had a white spot on his forehead. That's not normal in any picture of a fox I've ever seen. But, that one in the picture, he had that white spot, too. Askuwheteau told me to let the fox guide me, and to remind me to be careful. After I saw the fox in the picture, I closed my eyes and kind of focused my thoughts like I did during my vision quest. When I opened my eyes, everything was kind of hazy, like I was looking through a filmy window again. And, all of us—me, all of you, and Pa—were shining with bright colors that just kind of came out of us."

"Oh, my!" Maddie put her hand to her mouth.

"But there's more," Billy Mac said. "When I looked at Taregan, he didn't have that glow of color around him. He was surrounded by a black haze that kind of just clung to him. I mean as black as anything I've ever seen. Something about him just isn't right."

After a few moments of silence, Joseph was the first to speak. "That is very strange indeed. If we believe in the ability for some people to have this gift of vision, then we must believe, as Billy Mac does, that this man warrants scrutiny."

After a few more moments, Billy Mac broke the silence. "Well?" he asked, looking at each of his friends. One by one they all nodded.

"It doesn't hurt to be careful," Emmett said. "And watchful."

"Agreed," Maddie nodded.

"I believe that picture of the fox in the sheriff's office is too strange to chalk up to coincidence," Joseph said.

"Even though it has been there for a long time," Billy Mac acknowledged. "It's really weird, but it was what made me focus and have that vision again today. I really believe Taregan is bad news."

"I suggest we proceed with caution," Joseph said. "Agreed?" He put his hand out, palm down, into the middle of the group.

"Agreed," they all echoed. They each put their hands on top of Joseph's and gave a quick nod.

They broke up, and Emmett said, "Mackie and I are headed down to the construction site at the dam. Anyone else want to come along?"

"Can't," Joseph said. "Too much work to do."

"I can't, either," Maddie said. "Ma and Gramps are coming to town. Boomer and I need to wait for them."

"Okay," Emmett said. "We'll report back." He and Maddie exchanged smiles, and then he joined Billy Mac and Joseph on the front walk and they headed toward town.

Emmett and Billy Mac rode with Billy Mac's father in one of the town's few autos—one of the advantages of being sheriff. He was asked by the foreman at the construction site to come along with the professors from the university to look at the skeleton that was uncovered.

As they approached the worksite Billy Mac was startled by the pure scope of the project. He'd had no idea the amount of earth that had had to be moved to create the dam. It was massive. The equipment was amazing. Emmett—ever the know-it-all—explained that bulldozers had just been invented a few years prior. *Totally amazing,* Billy Mac thought. Especially the way the workers had to create a temporary channel to divert the river while the dam was being built. He could now understand the impression it had all made on Emmett and caused him to think about becoming an engineer. It was all very cool. He'd simply had no idea.

"How will they get the river to flow back into the riverbed when the whole thing's done?" Billy Mac asked. They were standing on a temporary levee.

"Dynamite," Emmett answered. "They'll blow the bluff above us here, filling in the channel, diverting the water back."

"Incredible!" Billy Mac said. "I'd like to be here to see that!"

"Probably not," Emmett laughed. "Anything close might get swamped in the rush of water!"

"Pretty impressive," the sheriff said. "Come on—let's go find the others."

"I can show you," Emmett said. "I know right where they are."

He led them to the far side of the project, then along a sandy path into a semi-circular grove of trees. They walked through the trees and found themselves in an open area, in a small alcove at the base of the bluff. Three men knelt on the ground, in conversation, as they studied what appeared to be old bones. At the sound of their footsteps, the men turned. One of the men stood up, looked at them, and a smile beamed.

"Principal Skinner!" Billy Mac exclaimed.

"Yes, yes," he replied as he walked over to them and shook hands with the sheriff. He turned to Billy Mac and Emmett and tilted his head back to look down through his glasses on the end of his nose. "Why am I not dumbfounded to discover you young charges at the locale of yet another cryptic situation? But where, pray tell, are your colleagues, Miss Miller and Mr. Noble?"

"Emmett's been working here," Billy Mac answered. "He wanted to show me the site, and the skeletons they'd found. Maddie and Joseph couldn't come."

"But what are you doing here, Principal?" Emmett asked.

"Alas, you forget. Hailing from Lafayette prior to my acquired position in our fair town, I was acquainted with these gentlemen. Being an authority on the aboriginal populace, with a fervent concentration on those of a resident nature, they implored me to join them. May I introduce Dr. Townsend, Professor of Osteology, and Dr. Murphy, Professor of Archeology, both of Purdue University?"

Introductions followed with handshakes, and everyone walked over to the area where the bones had been found in the sandy floor of the alcove.

"Did you think these are of a Native American, Principal?" Emmett asked. "Is that why you came?"

"As a vast multitude of artifacts has been recovered for eons in this region, it was thought likely. Observations thus far seem to confirm it as such."

"How did you find them, Emmett?" the sheriff asked.

"Several of us use this shady spot for our lunch breaks," Emmett explained. "I was sitting over there eating a sandwich." He pointed to a large, round, rock—about two feet wide. "We thought we saw something sticking out of the sand. We started scooping sand away, and before you knew it, there were a lot of bones. Some looked human; some looked like a few large dogs."

"There certainly are a lot," Dr. Townsend said. "At first glance, it appears to be an elderly male about five-foot-six, along with three wolves."

"Wolves?" Billy Mac gasped.

"Yes, son," Dr. Townsend went on. "From the damage done to some of the bones, and the way they are laid out, I'd say this elderly man had quite the battle on his hands with these wolves. They obviously killed him, but he went down fighting—taking three with him. Quite impressive."

"How old would you guess the bones to be, Doctor?" the sheriff asked.

"Seventy to a hundred years old. Once we have them in the laboratory, we may be able to be more precise. We'll contact the state. A proper team will map out the findings here, along with any other artifacts they uncover. Then everything will be properly transferred to the university for further analysis."

"Do you think the person was Native American, Doctor?" Emmett asked.

"A few artifacts we've found with the skeleton make me believe so. Principal Skinner?"

"I concur," he said. "They certainly appear to coincide with others of similar origin in our locality. Potawatomi, Shawnee, Wea, or Miami."

"All of which were present during the Prophetstown years," Emmett said.

"Precisely."

Billy Mac walked over to the large rock at the bottom of the bluff wall Emmett had pointed out and sat down. *It is a nice spot,* he thought. He tried to imagine how it would have looked decades ago, and the battle that had taken place between an elderly Indian and three wolves. It made him shudder. *But, why was he even here?* he wondered. Was he just going up or down the river and stopped for the night to make camp? If so, why here instead of by the river? He was likely traveling in a canoe. Why come all the way over here through the scrub to the bluff?

Billy Mac looked out into the grove of trees that sheltered the opening of the alcove, and then he saw it. Green eyes gazed at him through the undergrowth. A fox with a white spot on his forehead. It startled him at first, but then he remembered Askuwheteau's words again: "He will watch over you. Look to him for guidance." Billy Mac carefully looked around and saw someone watching them from a distance through the trees. He looked back at the fox, but he was gone. He looked back where he thought he'd seen a person, but there was nothing.

Chapter 14

After the meeting at the sheriff's office, Ahote went back to his campsite by the river. He was still stewing about Billy Mac.

The day before, he had scouted up and down the riverbank and found what he was looking for. At an abandoned cabin, he had found a canoe pulled up onto the shore. It was beat-up, but it was sound and watertight. It would give a way to easily move up and down the river.

He'd heard the kids talking about going to the worksite at the dam, and the sheriff, too. He'd follow and see what was going on. Probably had nothing to do with the gold, but he needed to keep a close eye on the kids—probably not the girl, just the three boys. Sooner or later, something would turn up.

He pushed the canoe into the river and floated downstream, hugging the shoreline to keep out of sight. It took a little longer than he thought, but he eventually saw signs of the worksite. He guided the canoe onto the sandy beach of a little natural cove, stowed the canoe behind some bushes, snapped a branch with some leaves off a bush, and wiped out his footprints. He'd had years of practice in covering himself.

Nobody was working on a Sunday afternoon. Still, he carefully wound around the quiet site, stopping here and there to listen. It didn't take him long to hear voices through the trees under the bluff. He crept through the trees, careful to stay off the path that had been made by the workers and careful not to step on any branches or leaves that would make sound. He peeked from behind a tree and there they were. The sheriff was talking with three men, all bent down and looking at something on the ground. The tall boy was with them. Then he saw the short kid—that Billy Mac kid that irked him so much—sitting on a large rock by the face of the bluff.

Suddenly, the kid looked straight at him and he quickly pulled his head back behind the tree. *Impossible!* he thought. There was no way that kid could have known he was out here! Rage crept over Ahote's twisted face. *What is it with that kid?* he wondered. Ahote swore under his breath, waited a few minutes, and quietly slipped off to wait for them to leave.

He found a large group of bushes by the wall of the bluff, hid behind them, and waited. Ten minutes later he could hear the group leave, talking and walking on the trail through the trees back to the worksite. It wasn't long before he heard the cars start up and drive away. Ahote waited a few more minutes, just to be safe, and then he walked to the alcove where the group had been.

A skeleton? he asked himself. *That's what they were here to look at?* He worked his way back to where he'd seen them gather, around the area of the bones, and sat on the large rock the boy had been sitting on. *So, it had nothing to do with the gold,* he thought, *but it's smart to keep an eye on them, whatever they do.* Those boys were bound to keep working on the mystery, and if they find the gold, he'd be there to jump on it. If the kids gave him any trouble, he'd jump on them, too.

Chapter 15

Billy Mac, Emmett, and Joseph sat on the large limestone outcropping by the creek below the Miller farm.

Billy Mac and Emmett had walked out to the farm from town on the railroad tracks, renewing their old contest about who could walk on the rails the longest without falling off. It seemed to Billy Mac to be the one thing he was better at than Emmett, and he couldn't help but let Emmett know it. His friend, good-naturedly, let him do so.

They'd left the tracks, walked down the bank off the railroad bed, through the thicket, and skirted the old cabin where they had originally found the ceremonial Indian pipe that started their adventures of last summer. Billy Mac paused to look through the front door of the cabin. Funny, he thought, it seemed so long ago. This was where the search for the gold all started.

He turned to follow Emmett to the creek, across the fallen tree that served as a bridge from one side to the other, then up onto the limestone outcropping that made such a perfect place to sit in the shade.

Joseph had ridden over on Henry, and the three of them talked while they waited for Maddie. Billy Mac turned to see her walking through the cornfield—now waist high—with Boomer bounding behind her. He smiled. Maddie was carrying her picnic basket. That meant fried chicken.

She sat down among them, spread a small tablecloth, and sat the basket in the middle. "Ya'll help yourselves," she said. "What are you talking about?"

"Thanks, Maddie," Emmett said, reaching for a drumstick. "Joseph's going down into that cave with Billy Mac."

"It seems the only thing to do at this point," Joseph said. "Askuwheteau told Billy Mac to look for the message that was left behind there. Perhaps there is some type of symbol or a sign of something I might pick up on, given my heritage and knowledge of The People."

The four friends sat, talked, and laughed while they ate. Billy Mac finished eating, got up, and walked along the creek bank, throwing sticks for Boomer to fetch. He'd grown to really like this spot, the creek lined on both sides by sycamores and cottonwoods. There always seemed to be a breeze through the creek bed, picking up the coolness of the water, then flowing up and over the bank. That breeze also rustled the leaves of the giant trees. Billy Mac couldn't think of a more pleasant place.

"Ready, Mackie?" Emmett called.

Billy Mac turned, walked back to the rock, sat down, then took off his shirt, shoes, and socks. Joseph had done the same. Emmett handed him the rope that was tied around a corner of the limestone ledge.

Billy Mac went down first. The water was still about waist high, and not quite as cold as it had been the first time he'd done this. In fact, it felt pretty good on a hot summer day. Joseph made his way down the rope along the facing of the rock, joined him in the creek, and then followed Billy Mac through the crevice in the rock wall into the small cave.

Thirty minutes later the four were sitting on the limestone outcropping. Billy Mac and Joseph were dripping wet. Billy Mac dried himself off with his shirt before he put it back on.

"I don't get it," Emmett kept saying.

"I don't either, Emmo," Billy Mac replied, irritated. "There's nothing down there. Go down and look for yourself."

"I didn't mean it that way, Mackie. Sorry."

"Billy Mac's right, though," Joseph said, putting his shirt back on. "We went over every inch of that sandy floor, feeling through the water with our hands, and every inch of the walls and roof of that cave. We even dug down into the sand to make sure the gold didn't simply sink down into it. There is nothing. No symbols, no sign of anything."

"If there's a message down there, it beats me," Billy Mac said. He hesitated and then said, "I think we need to talk about something."

Everyone looked at him. He was looking down at the limestone bolder they were sitting on, kicking at it with his foot.

"We need to all talk about whether we believe what happened to me was real," he said. "The vision I had with Askuwheteau."

"How come, Mackie?" Emmett asked.

Billy Mac finally looked up. "Because I saw the fox again. When I see it, I concentrate on what Askuwheteau told me, and it causes me to look for other things. Like it guides me, or gives me a hint to look for something, like a warning."

"When did you see it, Billy Mac?" Maddie asked.

"The other day down at the dam when I went with Pa and Emmett. I saw it looking at me through the brush. I thought about what Askuwheteau said in the vision, to let it guide me. So, I started looking around and I saw someone spying on us, hiding in the trees. I think it was Taregan. Not sure why I think it, but I do."

"Why didn't you say anything, Mackie?" asked Emmett.

"Because it kinda startled me. When I looked, again, they were gone—the fox and the person I saw watching us."

"But you really believe you saw them?" Joseph asked. "And, you really believe in the vision you had with Askuwheteau. Deep in your heart you believe?"

Billy Mac hesitated, then answered. "Yeah. In my heart of hearts, I believe the vision really happened. And, I believe what I saw down at the dam."

"I believe it, Billy Mac," Maddie said. She tilted her head and gave him a slight smile. "Let's not forget, when we were at the jailhouse you had that type of vision, again, when you could see the colors around us. I still don't understand it, but I believe you did it."

"I do, too," Joseph said. "It's a cornerstone of our heritage. The vision quests, and the guardians found in them, have guided countless numbers of people throughout our history."

They all looked at Emmett. He sat, looked off into the distance for a long minute, ran his hands over his face, and then turned to look at Billy Mac. His usual smile was gone. With a solemn nod of his head he said, "I believe, Mackie. We're all with you, one hundred percent."

Billy Mac forced a smile, a little embarrassed. "Thanks," he murmured with a quick glance at the other three. "But, what do we do? How do we keep an eye on Taregan if we think he's following us? And, why would he be following us, unless there's something bad about him? I really think there is."

They all sat in silence for a minute, each thinking of what to do. Suddenly Emmett jumped up. "I got it!" he exclaimed and smacked his hands together.

Everyone looked at him and waited for him to continue.

"The Baker Street Irregulars," he said. "That's what we need!"

"Emmett, what in the Sam Hill are you talkin' about?" Billy Mac asked him. Maddie and Joseph looked at Emmett quizzically.

"Come on—you know! The Baker Street Irregulars," he repeated, as if the others should know what he was talking about. He cocked his head and looked back at them in disbelief, then finally conceded. "Arthur Conan Doyle. The Sherlock Holmes stories. When Holmes needed eyes on the streets, he hired a rag-a-muffin crew of street boys—street urchins he called them. Gus and his gang will be our Baker Street Irregulars!"

Chapter 16

A couple evenings later, they all sat on the benches under the sycamore outside Joseph's blacksmith shop. Gus and his troupe stood in front of them, getting instructions from Emmett.

"That's all you want us to do, Emmett?" Gus asked. "Jest watch this guy an' let ya'll know what he does?"

Maddie always got tickled with Gus and the other boys. The rag-a-muffin description certainly fit. Most didn't wear shoes; most were in well-worn, patched overalls, some with no shirts. Tousled hair and a generous layer of smudge on their faces stood proof to their wrestling and whatever else they did to entertain themselves.

"That's right, Gus," Emmett answered. "Now, everyone, listen up. This is important. Don't get anywhere close to him. He might be trouble. We're not sure yet. Just keep an eye on him from a distance. And, you'll have to take turns doing it. That way, if he sees you, he won't see the same person hanging around all the time. He'll see a different person. He won't get suspicious."

"And jest report back to you er Joseph?" Gus asked.

"Yep," Emmett answered. "Either of us is fine. Just keep an eye on this guy for us. That's it. Now, what do you all want for payment?"

Gus poked the ground with a grimy toe, knitted his brows, and pursed his lips in thought. Then he turned to the other boys. "Andy?" he said to one of the boys. "What you want out of this?"

It didn't take the boy long to answer. "Aigs."

"Aigs?" Maddie asked.

"Yeah. Aigs. Me and Granny likes aigs. He raises 'em," the boy said and jerked a thumb at Billy Mac.

"Ohhhh," Emmett said. "Eggs. How many?"

"Half a peck."

Emmett quickly did the math and said, "Sure. No problem."

Gus looked at the next boy. "Jupe, what you want?"

The boy—his real name was Jupiter—answered quickly, too. "Frogs. I need two frogs. Jumpers."

"Done," Emmett said. He looked at a third boy. "Pete?"

"A shooter. A cat's eye shooter."

"You got it." Emmett looked at the last boy in the bunch. "Jasper?"

"Aw, heck, Emmett. I dunno!"

"We'll think of something," Emmett told him. "Don't worry." He turned back to the leader of the gang. "Okay, Gus. What do you want?"

Gus blushed through his freckles and motioned Emmett to come closer, then whispered in his ear.

Emmett stood up straight and smiled. "Yeah, sure. You bet."

Gus blushed, again, and turned to the boys. "Let's git. We got work ta do!"

They watched until the boys made the turn onto the street and Maddie busted out laughing. "Oh, my gosh," she said. "They're just too much!"

"They certainly are," Joseph agreed. "But they'll tell us what we need to know."

"What did Gus whisper to you, Emmo?" Billy Mac asked. "What did he want?"

"A kiss on the cheek from Maddie!" Emmett chuckled.

Maddie's eyes went wide, she raised her hands to her mouth and busted out laughing, again. "Oh, my gosh!"

And, the other three joined in.

Billy Mac tossed and turned on his back-porch cot.

"What's the matter, Mackie?" Emmett mumbled.

"Can't sleep. Too danged hot. Don't know how you can."

"It's not that bad. Lay still and you'll cool off."

"Emmo?"

"Yeah?"

"Do you think I'm crazy? All the stuff about the vision, the fox—all that stuff?" Billy Mac asked.

"No, Mackie. I told you, I believe in it. I believe you did it. What's wrong?"

"I don't know. Sometimes I wonder if it really happened or if I was just seeing things."

"What's your gut tell you? Think about it. Think about how it felt at the time. Then, ask yourself, did it really happen?"

They lay in silence for a few minutes. Billy Mac closed his eyes and tried to relax, as he did when he meditated for the vision quest. He could feel a bit of a cool breeze now. It flowed off the river and up over the bluff. Billy Mac could detect a hint of smoke. Someone along the river had a campfire going. And, he picked up the sweet smell of fresh-cut hay that had lain out in the summer sun all day.

"What's your gut tell you?" Emmett asked again.

Billy Mac opened his eyes and took a deep breath. "I think it was real," he finally said. "It changed me somehow. I don't see some things the same way anymore. I believe in things I didn't use to. And, it really bothered me at first thinking I had a guardian spirit looking after me. But now, I find it kinda comforting. It makes me feel good."

"Deep down inside?"

"Yeah, deep down inside," Billy Mac said.

"Then stop second-guessing it and second-guessing yourself. You'll drive yourself nuts. Don't worry about what anyone else might think. Grab hold of it. Let it be part of who you are. We believe in you. Believe in yourself."

Billy Mac looked up into the stars. Emmett was right, of course. He closed his eyes, focused into slow deep breaths, and again found the inner eye revealed to him during the vision quest. Calmness and joy embraced him. *It is who I am now,* he thought. *I am who I am.* Peace of mind and serenity flowed through his body and he could feel the energy in the belief of who and what he was.

Billy Mac opened his eyes again. Off in the distance he heard the whistle of the night train passing through a junction. It was a night sound he always found comforting, and he smiled.

"Thanks, Emmo. Night." He rolled over, closed his eyes, and fell asleep immediately, content in the conviction of his belief.

Chapter 17

Everyone had kept busy with their normal routines of chores and work. Billy Mac took care of the hen houses, the egg deliveries and weeded the garden. Once a week he swept out the jailhouse, took out the trash, and kept things straightened up. Summer was always a hectic time for Joseph—farmers were in constant need of repairs to be forged for equipment and horses had to be shod. Maddie finalized the room for her cousin, Becky, who would arrive soon. The painting and sewing were done—now she just needed to find the finishing touch of a pretty washstand with a mirror.

Emmett was spread between helping his mother at The Strand and working construction at the dam. The long-awaited movie projector had finally arrived. It had to be set up and someone trained on how to operate it. The whole town was anxious to watch Douglas Fairbanks as the Black Pirate revenge his father's death and, of course, win the princess at the end—

all in color, albeit still not a talkie. The projector would have to wait, though. The work at the dam was almost finished. In a few days, the blast crew would use dynamite to blow the river back into its regular channel. Emmett was driving Billy Mac nuts talking about it. He could hardly contain himself.

Gus and his troupe hadn't discovered much about Taregan. The boys had followed him when he was snooping around near Joseph's cabin, and even along the creek that bordered the Miller farm. So, it was obvious he was looking for something. They'd even watched him as he seemed to follow Emmett and Billy Mac around a few times. But he'd done nothing egregious yet. Still, it reinforced everyone's determination to be on their guard.

The four friends had decided they would meet at lunchtime every Saturday at Joseph's shop to talk things over and to determine if there was any new information that would help them with their mystery. Today was no different. Nobody had anything new to report. It looked like they were stuck.

Just as they were about to break up to go about their respective work, Billy Mac's father drove up, parked in the street, and walked up to them. It was evident something was wrong.

"Hey, Pa," Billy Mac said.

"Hey, son." He patted Billy Mac on the shoulder and nodded to the others. "Something's happened. Pete Keegan was out for a trail ride at the crossroads south of town, had his dogs with him. They took off into the woods. He followed on his horse and found a body.

The group all murmured their surprise. Maddie raised her hand to her mouth.

"Anybody report anyone missing?" Billy Mac asked.

"That's just it," the sheriff said. "Not only has no one in town reported anyone missing, but none of the sheriffs in the counties around us have contacted me about a missing person. That area's not too far from the railroad tracks, and normally I'd think it might have just been a hobo off the train, but there's something odd. The body didn't have any clothes on it."

Again, the group all expressed concern.

"So, there's nothing to identify who it is, Sheriff?" Emmett asked.

"Well, there is something. That's why I wanted to see Joseph."

"Me, Sheriff?" Joseph asked.

"If I told you the body had the tattoo of a feather on its upper arm, what would you say?" the sheriff asked.

"I'd say he was one of The People," Joseph answered. "It's a common tattoo among Native Americans."

"That's what I thought," the sheriff said. "I had a friend once. He was half Shawnee, and he had a tattoo of a feather."

"But, that's still not much to go on," Billy Mac said. "There must be thousands, maybe tens of thousands, of people with a tattoo of a feather."

"Well, there is something else," the sheriff said. "He had a second tattoo on his other shoulder. He was a marine. His tattoo was for the 2nd Division, 2nd Regiment of the Marine Corp."

"That should help narrow it down!" Emmett exclaimed.

"I'm going to contact some of the Native American councils," the sheriff said. "I'm also going to contact an old friend of mine who was a marine. He should be able to put me in touch with someone in the Marine Corp who can help look back through some records."

"Why don't you go talk with Taregan, Sheriff?" Maddie asked. "He could check right away with the Miami council of elders. And, he said they had close contacts with the elders of other tribes and nations, too."

"I would have done exactly that," the sheriff said. "But he's gone."

"Gone?" Billy Mac jumped up.

"Yes, he left earlier this morning. He came by the office and said he was going home, back to Peru. He said it didn't seem as if he was being of any help here. He thought he might be able to help more and do some research with their tribal members if he returned home. He promised to stay in touch."

Billy Mac sat back down. "That just doesn't make sense," he murmured to himself. "That just doesn't make sense at all."

They all talked a few more minutes, then the sheriff left. A few minutes later Gus and his gang came by to tell them Taregan's camp was empty. Emmett let them know the man had left town and discharged them of their duties, but promised to gather everything pledged to them and to get it to them as soon as he was able to.

"Everything?" Gus asked, and blushed.

"Everything," Emmett smiled.

Maddie covered her mouth and tried not to laugh.

Ahote finished setting up a new camp downriver from town, even a little farther south than the construction site for the dam. He'd found an isolated spot a few hundred yards off a gravel road in a wooded hollow. He'd hobbled the horse to a stake at the mouth of the hollow so it could graze in a circle, then set up camp farther back in the fold of the hollow next to a freshwater spring. There was no sign of human activity anywhere near. He'd be safe from prying eyes and it would allow him to move around freely, without being noticed.

He had decided the day before that his snooping around was getting nowhere and being camped in town jeopardized someone watching him as he did so. A few times he'd thought he'd seen a young kid following him, but he wasn't sure. So, he'd gone by the sheriff's office and played his false role to the hilt one last time—he'd told the sheriff he was going home but would continue his research with the elder council and promised to stay in touch. God, he was sick of playing the part of "the good Indian." Good riddance.

Maybe it was time for him to just take what he could and then clear out. He'd visited the sheriff's office enough times to know how to get in when no one was there. The back door from the alley could easily be jimmied. And he had a good sense of the sheriff's routine, when he came and went, when he did his rounds. He could slip in from the alley, spring the lock on the desk where the gold bar was kept and be out in a minute or two. He could live pretty good for a while. He still had some money left and the horse and wagon were in great shape. He'd just have to avoid the cities until he got out of the territory—people were bound to figure out before long that he'd been an imposter.

Yeah, that's what he'd do, he decided. Spend a few more days watching and waiting. If nothing new turned up, he'd hit the sheriff's office when the time was right, take that gold bar, and be long gone before anyone knew it.

Chapter 18

Two evenings later Billy Mac was sweeping the jailhouse. He'd followed his usual Monday night routine—he'd had dinner with his pa and then walked down to the jailhouse to sweep the floors and take out the trash. While he did so, his pa made his evening rounds, would subsequently meet him at the jailhouse, and they'd walk home together.

The phone rang and it startled Billy Mac. He wasn't used to it. They didn't have a phone at home and he'd only been in the jailhouse a few times when it was being used. *Should he answer it or not?* he wondered.

He hesitated, then walked to his father's desk, picked up the receiver part off the cradle on a candlestick-style black phone, and held it to his ear. A little apprehensively, he spoke into the mouthpiece. "Hello?"

"Billy Mac? Is that you?"

"Yes…"

"It's Maddie. Oh, my gosh, I'm glad you're there. I thought you might be. Is your father there?"

"No. He's making rounds. Are you all right? Where are you?"

"I'm home, at the farm. I'm fine, but Gramps is going to drive me into town. We'll stop and get Joseph on the way. Get Emmett and your dad. We'll meet you there at the jailhouse."

"Okay. Emmett's helping his ma over at The Strand. I'll get them both and meet you back here. Bye!"

Billy Mac stood there for a second wondering, and then jumped into action. As he headed out the door, he saw his father down the sidewalk a ways, routinely checking the doors of the shops as he passed them.

"Pa," he yelled. "Doc Miller, Maddie, and Joseph are on their way into town. They want to meet us here. I'm going to The Strand to get Emmett. We'll be right back!" His father waved back, and Billy Mac took off running toward the movie theater.

Not long afterwards they all crowded around the sheriff's desk. Doc Miller sat in the chair, his ever-present hickory cane by his side. It was that cane Doc had used to hit Ahote over the head last year to save Billy Mac from a certain beating.

"Thank you all for coming," the sheriff said. "But, what's up?"

"Beats me," Joseph shrugged. "Maddie wouldn't say until we were all here." He turned to look at her.

Maddie was all smiles. She tilted her head and brushed the bangs out of her eyes. "I was thinking about our mystery, and how things unfolded last year. Remember, we were stuck, and it turned out the answer was right in front of us all the time. Actually, it was right below us. As we sat on that creek bank all summer, what we were looking for—that cave—was right below us all the time."

"Sure," Emmett said. "But what are you getting at?"

"Sheriff, may I see that gold bar?" Maddie asked.

"Of course," he replied. He unclipped the ring from his belt, found the right key, unlocked the drawer, lifted the gold bar out, and handed it to Maddie.

"I was thinking about Askuwheteau's message to Billy Mac," she continued. "He told Billy Mac to look for the sign, the message that was left by his father, that would tell others where to look for the missing gold." She held the heavy bar up in front of her. "I think this is the sign, the message he left."

Everyone looked in silence at the gold bar. Finally, Emmett reached out and carefully took it from here. He turned it over a few times, looked at all sides, then handed it back to Maddie.

"It's like the sheriff said when we first looked at it—there are no markings on it, just a few scratches."

"Emmett," she said, "remember your Sherlock Holmes you were citing to us a few weeks back? He always said when you have eliminated the impossible, whatever remains…"

"…however improbable," Emmett concluded, "must be the truth." He turned the gold bar over again, squinted his eyes and studied it carefully. "Sheriff, do you have a piece of paper and a pencil?" he asked, still looking at the gold bar.

The sheriff reached into the top drawer of the desk, took them out, and handed them to Emmett. "Here goes," he said to everyone with a smile.

Emmett put the gold bar on the desk with the bottom facing up. He laid the paper on top of it, turned the pencil in his hand, and softly rubbed the side of the pencil lead back and forth over the paper to capture a clearer picture of the scratches. When he'd done the entire surface, he held the paper up for everyone to see, smiled again and twitched his eyebrows up and down a few times.

The rubbing captured much more than was apparent by simply looking at the gold bar. There were two specific points—probably created from a knife point—on each end of the gold bar, with a line from the first one intersecting a wavy line that eventually went down close to the other one.

"Well, I'll be." Doc Miller was the first speak. He leaned over for a closer look. "I'll be hanged if that isn't a map."

"Amazing," the sheriff echoed Doc. He took the paper from Emmett, looked at it, and then handed it to Maddie. "Simply amazing!"

Billy Mac and Joseph huddled around Maddie as the three of them looked at it.

"I suspect this first point…" Joseph pointed to the one at the top of the paper. "…is the original cave site. This line from it appears to be the creek, with all the proper twists and turns, running out and intersecting with the river. So, the other point is downriver. It has to be downriver because flipping the paper the other way would make the original point on the wrong side. So the bottom point has to be downriver."

"So, we just have to follow the river, make sure we know where we are with the various bends according to the map, and find the second point," Billy Mac said. "I can't believe it. You did it, Maddie! You solved it!"

"There's just one problem," Emmett said. Everyone turned to look at him. "The work at the dam is done. They've moved all the equipment out of the site. They're scheduled to blow the temporary channel with dynamite tomorrow, and the river will be back in its normal bed, flowing into the dam. Anything close to the riverbank is going to be under a lot of water—it's all going to be under a lake."

"Pa." Billy Mac looked at his father. "You're the sheriff. Can you get them to hold off?"

The sheriff scratched his chin. "Maybe. If needed, I might be able to get a court order, but I'd rather not do anything formal like that. It would create attention, which is what we don't want. I'll drive down to the dam at daylight to see if the foreman will work with me and hold off a day or two without me having to tell him why."

The phone rang, and it startled all of them. On the second ring the sheriff picked it up. He exchanged pleasantries, and then mostly listened. Every now and then he said "right," "okay," "got it," then he hung the earpiece back on the cradle.

He frowned and looked at everyone. "We have another problem. Remember I was going to call around to try and figure out the identity of that body? One of my first calls was to the sheriff in Miami County, where Peru is located. That was him calling back with information. He drove out to the reservation to speak with the elders to see if they were familiar with anyone that would have been a marine. Not only was Taregan in the 2nd Regiment of the 2nd Division of the Marine Corps, but they haven't heard from him since he left in his wagon to come visit us."

Maddie gasped. "That would mean…"

"Whoever that person was calling himself Taregan was an imposter," Billy Mac cut her off. "He'd told us he'd been in contact back and forth with the elders in Peru, but they're saying they hadn't heard from him. I knew there was something about that guy that bugged me!"

"It's worse than that," Emmett said.

"Right," the sheriff said. "It means that person—whoever he was—killed the real Taregan and left his body in the woods."

Doc took his cane and slowly stood up. "It appears, Sheriff, we have a dangerous man out there wandering around."

It was agreed Emmett and Billy Mac would wait at the jailhouse in the morning for the sheriff to get back from the construction site. If he was successful and the crew would hold off on the detonations, they'd borrow a canoe, head out onto the river and start matching the bends of the river with the diagram on the map. It was the only way to determine where that end point was that, hopefully, showed the location of the gold.

Joseph had work orders to get done and Maddie would stay at the farm. She could not convince her grandfather to let her go searching with Emmett and Billy Mac, not while there was a cold-blooded murderer running around the countryside. The sheriff couldn't go with Emmett and Billy Mac, either. He was going to have his hands full putting out an all-points bulletin to the surrounding counties, and then scouring their county for any trace of the imposter in case he was still close by.

Ahote scoffed. He'd heard the whole thing very clearly from the alley, standing below one of the jail cells' barred windows. He'd been waiting for everyone to leave.

Since nothing new had turned up the past few days, he had decided he would leave the territory. But he was determined to take that gold bar with him. He'd snuck into the alley behind the jailhouse at dusk. He had planned to force the back door open, break the lock on the desk, grab the gold bar, and be gone. He would have been in and out in less than two minutes, and he could have been ten or fifteen miles down the road before the sheriff went to the jailhouse in the morning and found the break-in. All he would have had to do was wait for the kid to finish his chores, for the stupid sheriff to make his rounds, and the two of them to have gone home together.

But, obviously, the discovery of the map on the gold bar changed things. The way he saw it now, he could keep an eye on the two boys and once they found the spot, move in fast. Or, he could still break in, take the gold bar, and use the diagram on it to find the hidden gold first. He'd been up and down this river a hundred times when he was a boy. He likely knew it better than they did and might be able to find the spot more quickly.

Instead of a quick break-in, he'd need to do it carefully, so no one saw the leftovers of an apparent robbery—a broken back door and a busted desk drawer. He was pretty good at picking locks, but it would take a while, maybe hours. If he could do it without leaving a trace, it's likely no one would even know the gold was missing for a few days. It was worth a try. After all, he had all night.

Chapter 19

It was midmorning the next day before Billy Mac and Emmett loaded their supplies into the canoe, shoved off, and headed upriver.

The sheriff had gotten the foreman to hold off on detonations until noon the following day. No amount of persuasion from the sheriff could get the foreman to stall any longer without consent from the utility company that financed the building of the dam—there were the demands of schedules and commitments to meet. The water had to start flowing through the dam. The foreman wasn't going to sacrifice his job by veering too much from the hard-and-fast deadline he'd been given.

With a known murderer on the loose, the sheriff had his work cut out for him. There was no way he could help Billy Mac and Emmett hunt for the treasure site, or spend more time trying to get the detonations at the site stalled further. It was up to them, but they only had a little over twenty-four hours. They'd search until dark, camp along the river, and start again at daybreak the next day. The sheriff made them both promise, multiple times, they wouldn't take any chances, avoid contact of any kind with any strangers, and be back in town—at the sheriff's office—before the dynamite detonations started.

It took an hour to reach the point upriver, north of town, where the creek from the Millers' farm ran into the river. It had been slow going against the current. It would be easier, and faster, now that they could head downriver, with the current.

A river is a funny thing. It's not static. Over periods of time, the shape of the riverbed can change. But it didn't take long before their map started to make sense. By midafternoon they'd made good progress and realized they could go faster and just match up the larger turns in the river with the map Emmett had made with his pencil rubbing. And, they could now gauge how much farther they had to go. So, they stopped the slower process of following the bank with every twist and turn, and headed downriver at full steam, both of them pumping with their paddles with Emmett in the front and Billy Mac in the back, steering with his paddle as needed.

By evening they'd come to the spot on the river adjacent to the second point on the map. Both boys were surprised to find they were at the construction site of the dam.

"Oh, my gosh, Mackie," Emmett said. They had paddled around a sharp bend into an area that opened into a sandy, horseshoe-shaped cove. They both got out and pulled the canoe onto the beach. "It was right here all the time. The whole time I was working down there. I could have walked right past it a hundred times!"

"We still don't know where it is, though," Billy Mac reminded him. "It could be anywhere."

"All we can do is walk in the direction the map shows," Emmett said and pointed toward the bluff. "It's going to be dark soon. Let's do a quick look-see, and then we can come back and set up camp."

They worked their way through bushes, vines, and undergrowth and eventually came to a familiar spot—a grove of trees guarding the little alcove into the bluff wall.

"Of course, Mackie! It all makes sense. That skeleton might have been Askuwheteau's father. He might have brought the gold here but was got caught by wolves. That gold should be in there, somewhere."

They walked through the trees into the clearing of the alcove. They looked for signs scratched onto the bluff wall, on trees, or any sign of a marker on the ground. Nothing.

"Emmo, it's getting too dark to see. There could be something right in front of us, and we'd miss it. Let's go set up camp and eat something. I'm starving. We can get a start at daybreak."

Emmett agreed and they trudged back to the beach. They built a small, smoky fire to keep the bugs away, ate a cold supper, then plopped down on top of their sleeping bags. Both were exhausted from a day of paddling.

"Nice out here away from town," Billy Mac said. "Sky is so full of stars. Amazing."

"Yeah," Emmett agreed. "The glow of lights in town sometimes makes it hard to see all the stars. Or, when the moon's out. The glow lights up the sky too much."

"Wish there was a moon out tonight," Billy Mac said. "We could keep on looking around if there was." He lay in silence for a minute and listened to the multitude of bullfrogs from up and down the river. "Emmo, do you really think we'll find the gold?"

"Don't know, Mackie. I believe it's out there. We know from Skinner and those guys from the university that the skeleton we found was of an old Indian. And, that skeleton is right where the map shows the gold was moved to. I think it has to be there, somewhere. Just wish we had more time to look for it before the blasting starts and this all becomes the bottom of a lake."

"Once they blast, how long will it take for the water to rush in?"

"I asked the foreman once. He says there's no way to know for sure. The initial rush could be pretty strong, especially with all the rain they've had farther up north. All that water is rushing downriver and the current in the river is stronger than normal. But it really depends on the new surface area. The dam will push the river up into the shore, back up into the creeks, and create coves that will wind back through the hills. So, it just depends on how wide the new lake will be. Then, after the first twenty feet or so, it will keep getting deeper, but not as fast. It could even take years before the water finally levels off at about forty feet deep down here by the dam."

"Okay. Up at first light then. We'll have to work fast to be out of here before the blasting starts. Night, Emmo."

"Night, Mackie."

It was maddening to be so close but still so far out of reach. *How could they search everywhere they needed to in the few hours they had left?* Billy Mac closed his eyes, listened to the sounds of the river, and drifted into a restless sleep.

He stumbled through the brush and squinted through the haze. Every now and then he could glimpse the figure of an old man with long gray hair dressed in a leather tunic and leggings. The old Indian would stop, turn, and beckon Billy Mac to follow, and then walk a little farther, turn, and wave again. Then Billy Mac saw it—the fox at the feet of the old man— waiting and watching Billy Mac with those deep green eyes. They both disappeared into the grove of trees outside the alcove. Billy Mac followed them through the trees into the opening. The full skeleton of a man dressed in a leather tunic and leggings sat cross-legged in the middle of the alcove. Billy Mac looked through the haze and saw the fox sitting on the same large rock by the cliff wall that he had sat on weeks before when he and Emmett had visited the site. Billy Mac looked back at the strange apparition of the fully clothed skeleton sitting in the sand, but he'd vanished. He looked back at the fox, but it was gone, too.

Not far away, Ahote bedded down. Those boys had found this spot faster than he had hoped. He'd followed the diagram on the gold bar and made it to the construction site by midafternoon. He'd beached his canoe, hid it in the brush, wiped out his footprints in the sand with a branch of leaves, and then started looking around. He'd wanted more time by himself before they got here.

Once he'd heard them, he'd followed them from a distance, saw them go through the trees into the alcove at dusk, and saw them come out a short while later. It was obvious they hadn't found anything. He hadn't, either. He'd gone to the same spot before they'd gotten here, reached the same obvious conclusion that the remains of the skeleton might have been the person that hid the gold. If that was true, that meant the skeleton was his grandfather. So what? He'd cared nothing for his father—had actually hated the man. Why would he feel differently about a grandfather?

He'd be up at the crack of dawn. He could do his own looking around for clues and keep an eye on those kids from time to time. Maybe by this time tomorrow night he'd be rich.

Chapter 20

"And they just disappeared?" Emmett asked. Billy Mac had told Emmett about his dream from the night before as they walked through the trees, back into the little clearing at the base of the bluff.

"Yeah. I followed them through the trees into here. There was a complete skeleton with Indian clothes on it, sitting cross-legged right there," he said, pointing to the ground in the middle of the alcove. "The fox was sitting on that big rock over there by the cliff. Then they both just disappeared."

"Do you think it was a sign? More than just a dream? Maybe their spirits reaching out to you again?"

"Beats me. If it was, then they purposely wanted me to come in here. Askuwheteau said to let the fox guide me. So, I'm going to start over by that rock on the corner of the cliff and look for any kind of marker or sign of a message in the wall.

You start over on the other side, on the other corner. We'll meet in the middle."

They spent an hour checking every inch of the cliff face, from the ground to seven feet up. Nothing. Then they each went back to the corners of the alcove and followed the cliff face around out of the clearing for another twenty yards in both directions. Still nothing.

Ahote had watched them earlier from afar as the boys had gone through the trees into the alcove. If the construction crew was going to use dynamite today, they didn't have a lot of time. He'd let the kids look for the gold in that recessed area along the cliff and he'd look elsewhere. He'd check on them from time to time and stay within shouting distance. If he heard them whooping it up because they found something, he'd move in fast. He smiled an evil thought. Even if they didn't find anything, he might still give them a little payback for all the grief they'd caused him.

Back in the alcove, Billy Mac sat on the big rock at the bottom of the wall. He took his cap off, wiped the sweat from his face with his shirt, and leaned against the cliff face. The rock wall was nice and cool against his sweaty back.

"I don't get it," Emmett said. He plopped down in the sand next to Billy Mac. "We have to be missing something."

"You don't think he would have buried it?" Billy Mac asked.

"I don't think so. By all accounts, he was an old man. Digging would be hard on an older person. Besides, they hid it in a cave the first time. It makes sense he would have done the same thing the second time."

"No cave close to here," Billy Mac said. He stood up, walked to the front of the alcove, and looked into the trees. Emmett got up and followed him. "Looks like we struck out. We're gonna have to leave here before long."

Billy Mac turned around for one last look at the alcove and was shocked by what he saw. "Emmo!" he said, pointing to the rock.

"What, Mackie?" Emmett asked and looked around. Billy Mac was speechless, pointing. "What?" Emmett asked again.

"You don't see that?"

"See what, Mackie?"

"The fox sitting on the rock. Right there!"

"I don't see anything! You mean you see him?"

"Yeah! He's right there!"

"I can't see him, Mackie. Swear I can't."

Billy Mac got hold of himself. "Look to him for guidance," Billy Mac murmured Askuwheteau's words to himself. He stared at the fox, which peered back at him with his green vixen eyes. "Right where he was sitting in my dream last night," he mumbled. Then the fox jumped down and went to the edge of the tree line and sat, peering outward.

Billy Mac looked back at the rock the fox had been sitting on. "Emmett—it's that rock. It has to be," he said and walked over to it. "We have to move this rock over. There's either something on it we can't see or something behind it. Help me!"

They each got on the far side and pushed. It didn't give. They dug at the base of it all the way around. It was bigger than it looked, having settled into the sand like it was. Little by little they made progress. Finally the rock slowly gave way. With much effort they rolled it over and found themselves looking at the mouth of a small cave opening.

"Mackie! Woohoo!" Emmett whooped a few times and Billy Mac joined in, their shouts echoing off the walls of the bluff around them.

Just then, an explosion shook the ground. The force of the shock waves reverberated through the trees and threw the boys off balance. Some rocks and dirt above them on the bluff broke away and fell around them.

"Emmo! They're blasting!"

Emmett looked at his watch. "But they aren't supposed to start for another hour!"

"Well, they're doing it now. We have to work fast!"

Billy Mac got down on the ground and tried to work his way through the opening. He couldn't get very far—he was too big. The opening had filled in with sand and silt over the decades from multiple floods. "I can see it opens up a little ways farther. There's not much light with me stuck in here like I am, but I can see there's kind of a glow. It looks like there's something in there!"

A noise behind him sounded like a stick hitting a rock, and then a thud with something falling to the ground.

"Emmo?" Billy Mac called. "What was that noise?"

Someone grabbed his legs and pulled him viciously backwards out of the opening. Billy Mac clawed to get a hand on something to catch himself but found nothing. Back out in the open he quickly rolled over, stared into the face of Ahote bending over him, and froze. Flashbacks of that terrible face from last summer during their struggle in the riverbed came back to him instantly.

"You!" Billy Mac yelled.

"Yeah, me," Ahote scowled. "And that noise was your friend getting hit on head." He held the gold bar up in front of him. "That's right—I took it from the sheriff's office. You fools didn't know I heard everything the other night from outside the back window. Well, now I'm gonna get what's mine."

Billy Mac looked at Emmett, sprawled in the sand unconscious.

"You're gonna help me with what you found, and you're not gonna give me any trouble or you'll get the same as him, or worse," Ahote said, jerking his head toward Emmett's body.

Billy Mac froze for a few seconds and then yelled as loudly as he could, "Help! Help me!" His shouts echoed off the cliff walls that surrounded the alcove.

Ahote bent farther down, savagely grabbed him by the throat with his left hand to choke off his yelling, and then hit him in the face repeatedly with a right-handed fist. "Now shut up," he said, and pushed Billy Mac's head into the sand.

There was a loud growl as an animal raced through the trees behind them. Billy Mac forced open his beaten left eye, glanced through a dizzying haze, and saw Boomer sprinting toward them. The dog leapt onto Ahote and knocked him off Billy Mac. Man and dog wrestled, rolling over and over in the sand, Boomer biting and snapping, Ahote trying to push him off with his arms and legs. Finally, there was a loud yelp and Boomer went still. Ahote panted several times, caught his breath, and then forced himself to his feet. His arms were lacerated with bites and he gripped a bloody knife in his right hand.

He stumbled toward Billy Mac, his face a horrible thing to see. "Now you....," he started.

"Hold it right there!" Billy Mac knew the voice of his father and he lay back into the sand, relief spreading through him. "Don't move!"

The sheriff's gun pointed at Ahote, but the criminal already had Billy Mac. He'd tossed the gold bar aside, grabbed Billy Mac by the hair, and jerked him off the ground, his other hand holding the knife across the boy's throat.

"Don't you move, Sheriff, unless you wanna make this worse," Ahote grunted.

Behind the sheriff, Maddie and Joseph ran from the trees into the clearing, saw what was happening, and stopped in their tracks.

Maddie saw Boomer's lifeless body a dozen yards away by the cliff, ran to it, and threw herself on him, sobbing. She turned to Ahote, still holding Billy Mac's head by the hair of his head, the knife at his throat. "Murderer! You murderer!" she choked out.

"Don't move, girl!" Ahote shot back and jerked Billy Mac's head back viciously.

"Maddie, don't move," the sheriff said, not taking his eyes off Ahote. "You okay, son?"

"Yes, Pa," Billy Mac gasped back. "Not sure about Emmett." Billy Mac was still dizzy from the beating. He found it hard not to black out, and it was hard to see out of his swollen left eye.

"Joseph, see to Emmett," the sheriff said.

Joseph held his hands up in front of him so Ahote could see there was no threat. He slowly walked over to Emmett and bent down to check him. "He'll be okay, Sheriff. Big lump on his head and a little bleeding, but he's breathing steady." He lifted Emmett's head, slightly tapped him on both cheeks, and the boy slowly opened his eyes, mumbling something groggy.

"He's awake, now," Joseph said, and then mumbled something back to Emmett. He pulled him toward the rock wall and propped him up.

It was quiet and still except for Maddie sobbing over Boomer.

"Here's how this is gonna work, Sheriff," Ahote broke the silence. "I'm taking this boy with me. You move over there with them." He jerked his head toward Maddie, Joseph, and Emmett. "We're gonna take your car. You're all gonna wait here until you hear me blow the horn, then you're gonna wait for another ten minutes before you leave here. If I see anyone come out of those trees back to the worksite, I'll slit this boy's throat from ear to ear, and I know how to do it. Do you understand me?"

The sheriff slowly nodded.

"Say it!" Ahote demanded.

"I understand. Now you understand me, if you harm that boy anymore, in any way, I'll hunt you down and kill you myself."

"Get outta the way," Ahote growled. "Over there," he said and jerked his head toward the others.

The sheriff moved over to Maddie, Joseph, and Emmett, who was propped against the rock wall.

Ahote backed his way to the trees, dragging Billy Mac backwards with him. Once they got to the trees Ahote turned and quickly pushed Billy Mac ahead of him. "I got this knife ready to go into your spine if you make a bad move," he grunted.

They left the trees and moved out into the worksite. There were no workers or equipment—everyone and everything was gone.

They worked their way to the far side of the dam to the sheriff's car. There was another worksite truck next to it. Ahote tightened his grip in Billy Mac's hair, dragged him to the truck, and reached down and punctured a tire with his knife. He then dragged Billy Mac around it and punctured the other three. He pushed Billy Mac to the sheriff's car, opened the driver's side door, and pushed Billy Mac through to the far side. "Don't be stupid, boy," he glanced at Billy Mac. "I can slice you up just as easy from here." Billy Mac crouched away and turned his beaten, bloodied face toward the door.

Ahote started the Model T and drove to the top of the ridge. He stopped and let the car idle for a minute, then reached out and honked the horn three times. The sound echoed up and down the river. He put the car back into gear, drove out onto a county road, and turned south. They drove for perhaps five minutes, Billy Mac still turned away into the door. As they neared a sharp bend, Ahote maneuvered the curve, reached over, opened the passenger door, pushed Billy Mac out, accelerated out of the bend, and drove away.

Billy Mac rolled over and over as he tumbled down the bank into a ravine, finally stopped by the brush and his head hitting a tree. He tried to move but the pain in his face and head was too much and he blacked out.

The sound of voices and someone scrambling down the bank into the ravine brought him back around. A few moments later someone was wiping his face with cool water, lifting his head up. Billy Mac opened his good eye and looked up into the freckled, disheveled face of young Gus.

Chapter 21

Billy Mac drank some water from Gus's canteen and managed to tell him that his father and the others were back at the construction site. He worked his way into a sitting position against a tree and waited for the dizziness to subside. While he did so, Gus went back up to the road and gave instructions to one of the boys, who hopped on his bike and sped away back toward the dam.

His head finally cleared, Billy Mac slowly stood up, holding onto a tree to make sure the dizziness wouldn't come back. He worked his way up to the road, rested for a moment, and then started walking down the road toward the dam and town. Gus and two other boys walked their bikes beside him.

A short while later they could see the temporary work crew road that led off to the dam's worksite. There at the top of the road were his father and his friends. Joseph had carried Boomer's body and laid it in the grass, Maddie bent beside it.

The sheriff ran to Billy Mac and hugged him. "You all right, son?" he asked, then held him away so he could survey the damage to Billy Mac's face.

Billy Mac nodded, looked to his friends, and walked over. He knelt beside Maddie and hugged her. "I'm so sorry, Maddie," he managed, tears running down his mangled face. He stroked Boomer's head as he had always done. "He saved me, Maddie. He saved me," and the tears flowed again. Joseph and Emmett both walked over, and they all huddled in their grief.

Several minutes later Billy Mac stood up and walked back over to his father, who was standing with Gus and the other two boys. They sat down in the shade.

"I don't understand, Pa," he said. "How did you know where we were? Why were you even out there?"

"I'd been out all morning talking with folks in the county to see if they'd seen that imposter—now we know it was Ahote—driving his wagon. You and Emmett were supposed to be back at the jailhouse before lunchtime, so I went back there to see if you'd found anything. Of course, you weren't there, but Maddie and Joseph were. They were waiting for you. When they got there, they'd found a note stuck to the door from the foreman of the construction crew that they were going to start blasting earlier than he'd promised me. As soon as I got there, they showed the note to me, and we jumped in the car to get out here as fast as we could.

"As we drove up, we heard the first blast go off. We got to the workers before they could do another one and I made them halt operations for the rest of today. They weren't very happy with me, but the foreman eventually told the crew to quit and they all left for the day. We started looking around and I remembered that spot where the workers found that skeleton. We had already started toward that area when we heard you yell for help. Boomer took off through the trees like lightning and we followed. You know the rest."

"I'm sure glad you did," Billy Mac said, then looked at Gus. "But what were ya'll doing out here?"

"Well, we was in town and heered the sheriff talkin' to Miss Maddie and Joseph like there was trouble. They jumped in that car and took off lickety split. Couple of us had bikes and we jumped on 'em and followed best we could. Got close, down yonder way, and saw that car come tearing back up out onto the road with a different fella drivin' and you in there, too. Didn't look right to us, so we kept on followin' till we saw you laying down there a moanin' in that brush."

"Thanks, Gus. Sure glad you did, too." Billy Mac looked around then asked his father, "But where's Jasper? Gus sent him back to find you."

"I sent him to town to get Joseph's father," the sheriff said. "Looks like him coming now. We'll get back to town for another car, take Maddie home, and have Doc take a look at you and Emmett. Then I'll get some men together and we'll start combing the county to see if we can find any trace of Ahote."

The sheriff looked at Gus and the other two boys. "I owe all of you my thanks. If I can ever be of help to you, you know where to find me." He went to each and shook their little hands, which somewhat embarrassed them.

Thomas Noble drove up in his wagon. Joseph carefully laid Boomer in the wagon bed behind the bench seat, and then the four friends all worked their way in around him. The sheriff climbed up sat on the bench seat next to Thomas, who then released the handbrake, snapped the reins, turned the wagon around, and started toward town.

Chapter 22

Doc Miller had checked them both over. Emmett had a mild concussion from the blow on the head and was told he must remain fairly inactive with no exertion for at least twenty-four hours. No ifs, ands, or buts.

Doc thought Billy Mac might have a hairline fracture on his cheekbone where Ahote had struck him three or four times with his fist. The swelling and bruising would last several days, and some blood vessels had burst in his left eye. He looked ghastly.

They'd all decided to meet at Joseph's shop the next day at noon. Everyone was already there sitting on the benches when Billy Mac walked up, Boomer's absence evident.

As he walked up, Maddie rose to meet him, silently put her arms around him, and gave him a long hug. She took his hand and led him over to a bench to sit down with her and Emmett.

"I'm so sorry, Maddie," Billy Mac said awkwardly. She squeezed his hand in quiet acceptance.

"We'll be okay," she said after a few moments. "Gramps and I buried him this morning down by the creek. He always loved to play in and out of the brush down there. I'll plant some flowers in a day or so."

They all sat in silence for a minute, then Emmett tried a little levity. "Mackie, I didn't think that left side of your face could look worse than last night. Guess I was wrong." He tried a lopsided smile.

Billy Mac appreciated the change of subject and played along. "Yeah, I know. Last night it was just purple. Today there's some nice shades of green and red, too." He tried to smile but winced at the pain it caused.

"Too bad it's not Halloween," Emmett said. "We wouldn't even have to make you up for it. I believe you could scare the whiskers off a cat."

"Does it hurt bad?" Maddie asked, softly touching his cheek.

"Not too bad," he lied, and winced again.

"So, where are we with all this?" said Joseph, asking the obvious question.

"Pa's car was found a ways down south of the dam not far from some railroad tracks. Ahote must have abandoned it knowing there'd be people out searching for it. Pa thinks he might've jumped a train to get out of the county unseen."

"They are going to start blasting at the dam again tomorrow morning," Emmett said. "There are a lot of people pushing to get it finished and water flowing through the turbines. There are crews waiting to run power lines for the electricity it's going to generate. A lot of people have their reputations, and money, on the line."

"We still don't know if there's anything down there, do we?" Maddie asked. Everyone looked at Billy Mac.

"I have to admit, we don't," he said. "If we'd only had a few more minutes, we'd know for sure." He closed his eyes and fought to recall what he saw, and didn't see, looking into that cave. "I felt like I could see...something. Not like anything solid or anything stacked up. But, the little bit of light that got into that cave kind of made it...glow. That's the only way I know how to say it. I just feel like something has to be in there."

"But there are a lot of minerals that could give off a glowing reflection," Emmett said. "Sandstone can do it. And, especially pyrite, what people call Fool's Gold. It's in the ground around here everywhere."

"I don't think the fox spirit would have led me into that opening through the trees," Billy Mac said, "and then sit on that rock to coax me to move it unless there was something in there. That glow I saw was golden."

"Not disagreeing with you, Mackie, just naming possibilities."

"No one is ever going to know until someone goes down there," Joseph said.

"No one is getting down there now," Billy Mac said. "Pa says the construction company has armed guards to keep anyone from going anywhere near the site until they're done blasting."

"What does your dad say about it all?" Maddie asked.

"He says he has to agree with the construction company. There's a murderer running around and there's no proof there is anything down there. As the sheriff, he says the safety of the community comes first, no matter what we believe—or want to believe—is down there."

"I can't say I disagree," Maddie said as she wiped a tear from her cheek. The loss of Boomer was going to be hard to deal with for a long time.

"Look here," Joseph said and nodded toward the street.

"Our Baker Street Irregulars," Emmett said. "They really helped us out and saved the day. I asked them to meet us here."

While the other boys looked their normal selves, Gus was all cleaned up. Clean overalls and clean white shirt underneath. He didn't have shoes on, nor was his hair slicked back with the pomade that Vacation Bible School had demanded, but his face was clean and there had been an obvious attempt to comb his hair. He led the boys up the path. He held his hands behind his back in an attempt to conceal some flowers.

"Joseph, Emmett, Billy Mac," he said and nodded to each of them. "Miss Maddie," he said and blushed. And, for the first time that day, Maddie smiled.

"All of us want to thank all of you," Emmett said earnestly. "You did more than we asked—way more. I don't know if we'll ever be able to say thanks enough. At the very least, we want to keep our promise." He stood up, turned around, bent over, reached behind the bench, and lifted a metal pail, a shoebox with a string tied to keep it shut, and a smaller box from the ground. He sat each on the bench.

He decided where he should start, picked up the pail, and turned toward the boys. "Andy, a half-peck of eggs," he said and handed it to him. "I hope your granny makes you something really good with them."

He picked up the shoebox, turned, and handed it to another boy. "Jupiter, the best two jumpers I could find. Got them myself from the creek this morning." The boy undid the string, lifted the lid a little to peek, and the largest frog Billy Mac had ever seen shot out of the box, knocking the top all the way off. It hit the ground jumping in giant leaps. The second frog followed suit in a different direction. The boys all scrambled to catch them. Andy's bucket of eggs got knocked over and he hovered over them to keep them from getting stepped on. It took all five boys several minutes to corral the two jumpers back into the shoebox. Gus had dropped the handful of wildflowers he'd brought for Maddie during the mayhem and had to gather them back up, some the worse for wear. He shyly hid them behind his back again. Everyone had a much-needed laugh.

Everything calmed down and Emmett picked up the small box. "Pete, the finest cat's eye shooter I ever had," he said as he handed it to the boy. "It never let me down. It doesn't miss." The boy opened the box and looked wide-eyed at the perfect oversized marble lying on a bed of cotton. The others crowded around and murmured approval.

"Jasper," Emmett said. "I told you we'd think of something." He turned, bent back behind the bench, and picked up a long, skinny package wrapped in butcher paper and handed it to the boy. "My old trusty model-H Daisy repeater. Holds three hundred and fifty shots. There's still a bunch in there." The boy carefully tore the paper packaging away and stood there speechless, the air rifle reverently cradled in his hands. He shook it a little so he could hear the lead shot rattling around in the magazine chamber. His friends all patted him on the back, murmuring "good job," "ain't that a dandy," and "cain't wait to try it."

"Gus," Maddie called to the young hero with a smile. She held her hand out. The boy walked over to where she sat on the bench and held the flowers out to her. She graciously accepted them and laid them on the bench next to her. Then, she took his hand in both of hers and said, "Thank you for helping my friends. I'll always be grateful, and I'll always be proud to be your friend." She then gently reached up, held his head, kissed him on each cheek, and a third time on the top of his unruly head. "Thank you," she said again.

Instead of blushing, Gus smiled back, stood a little taller, then turned to his crew and said, "All right boys, let's git to checkin' these things out!" He walked off with the rest of them, a new little swagger in his step.

"Good job, Emmo," Billy Mac said.

"Yes. That was really nice of you, Emmett," Maddie said. "They certainly deserved it."

"You're going to have to be careful, Emmett," Joseph said. "I believe 'Miss Maddie' has a new suitor!"

This time Emmett blushed, and they all busted out laughing, again.

Billy Mac and Emmett lay on their cots on Billy Mac's back porch. All the stars were out and a cool breeze brought a welcomed respite to what had been a hot summer. Cooler weather also meant a new school year was close upon them. A change of pace might be nice, Billy Mac thought. The usual night sounds rose and fell with the sweet smell of honeysuckle in the air.

"How're you feelin', Emmo?"

"Pretty good. Just about normal. You?"

"The aching has pretty much stopped. Just hurts if I press on the side of my face."

"Don't press on it."

"Right." Billy Mac paused for a minute. "Emmo, there's something I need to tell you."

"Yeah?" Emmett was sounding sleepy.

"The other day at the dam, when Ahote attacked us, I should've known. I could have kept it from happening."

That woke Emmett up. He sat upright. "But that's crazy, Mackie. How could you have stopped it? There was no way to know."

"If I had paid attention I would've. Remember I saw the spirit of the fox on that rock, just like in my dream, right?

That's what made me realize there was something special about that rock. When the fox jumped down, he went to the edge of the trees and sat there looking out. I didn't pay any more attention to him 'cause I was so focused on moving that rock and finding treasure. I let it cloud my judgment."

"What do you mean, Mackie?"

"In my vision, Askuwheteau told me the fox would watch over me, that I should seek guidance from him. That I should become clever and aware like him to help me avoid danger by accepting his guidance."

"So?"

"So, when he jumped off the rock, went to the edge of the trees, and sat there looking into them, I should have known something bad was out there. I let the excitement of finding treasure take over. I wasn't clever. I wasn't following the guidance of my guardian spirit."

"You're putting too much on yourself," Emmett said and lay back down. Then, like always, he tried to inject some levity. "Don't beat yourself up—someone already did that for you."

"But Emmett. You got hurt bad. You could have been killed by the blow on your head from that bar of gold! I'm so sorry!"

"Mackie, it's okay. I'm okay. You're okay. Let's leave it at this—the next time you see the fox, we'll pay attention. We'll think twice, maybe three times, before jumping into something. Deal?"

"Deal." Billy Mac felt better after talking about it. Emmett forgave him, but it would be a long time before he'd be able to forgive himself for allowing his friend to be hurt.

"You know, Mackie, I've been thinking."

Uh-oh, Billy Mac thought. "About what?" he asked cautiously.

"Well, they're going to do the detonations tomorrow afternoon. Why don't we get Joseph to drive us in the wagon across the bridge to the bluff on the other side of the river, and then follow the road down to where we can watch?"

"How come?"

"I'd like to pinpoint that alcove and cave spot from up on that far side of the bluff. Once the lake gets to full level it might be hard to know exactly where it is."

"How come?" Billy Mac asked again.

"Someday we may be able to get back down there. Deep-diving equipment has been around almost ten years now, according to *Popular Mechanics*. A hose runs down from the surface, through the water, and they pump air into a helmet on a diving suit. A person can breathe just fine. They use it for underwater salvage and stuff."

"No kidding?"

"Yeah. And, I read an article that two guys in France are working on a tank kind of thing that straps to your back with a hose that runs to a mask you put over your face that would actually let you swim underwater for a while. So, who knows what we might be able to do at some point down the line? But we'd have to know where to look. We need to mark that spot. We can do that from the bluff on the other side of the river."

"We're not gonna to do anything stupid, like try to go down there?"

"Gosh, no! We promised Doc, and your pa, we'd take it easy for a few days."

"Okay. We'll go see Joseph in the morning. Night, Emmo."

"Night, Mackie."

Miles south, Ahote had holed up at the campsite he'd set up deep within the hollow days before. He'd decided it would be too risky to travel the roads or even hop a train. There would be bulletins about him sent over the wires to all the surrounding counties, maybe even statewide. Best to just hunker down out of sight a day or so and let the chance of being caught die down. He didn't even have a fire going, afraid someone might smell the smoke.

He'd ditched the sheriff's car a few miles away by the railroad tracks. *That might throw them off,* he thought. They might think he'd hopped a train and focus their search elsewhere. That would make it easier and buy him some time.

He couldn't stop thinking about the gold. If he still had that one gold bar he'd stolen from the sheriff's office he'd be content and not worry about the rest of it that might be in that cave. He could still make out pretty well with the horse, wagon, and its contents.

But he didn't have it. He'd tossed it aside during the showdown with the sheriff and forgot to pick it back up when he dragged that kid out of the construction site. Likely it had fallen out of sight when he tossed it, or else he would have seen it, remembered it, and picked it back up. Maybe the sheriff and those other kids didn't think about it, either. They were probably tending to the boy he'd knocked out. *That gold bar is probably still laying there.*

He couldn't go back through the normal entrance to the site—someone was bound to see him. But maybe he could skirt around it on the other side of the river along the bluff. Maybe he could find a way to slip down, get it, and get back out. *Yeah,* he thought. *It's worth a try.* He could take the canvas cover off the back of the wagon so it wouldn't attract attention and use some old clothes and an old hat to disguise himself, somewhat. It wasn't that far away, and if he traveled just after sun-up, he should be fine. Satisfied with his decision, he climbed into the back of the covered wagon, rolled onto the pallet of blankets, and fell right to sleep.

Chapter 23

Billy Mac promised his pa they'd be back at the jailhouse as soon as the blasting was over. They were simply going to ride with Joseph, in his wagon, to watch it all happen from the bluff across the river. The sheriff wasn't convinced until Emmett offered that they probably wouldn't even get out of the wagon. They'd probably be able to see just fine from the wagon bench, because he'd brought the binoculars he'd ordered from the Sears & Roebuck Company last year. Besides, Maddie was meeting her cousin, Becky, at the train station at three o'clock that afternoon. The boys had promised Maddie they would meet the girls back at the jailhouse for introductions.

Billy Mac's father reluctantly agreed that it might be interesting to watch the blasting and the river rush in. He even said he'd go with him if he wasn't so busy with the manhunt for Ahote. He finally consented with a double warning, extracting promises from both of the boys, again.

Joseph snapped the reins, guided the wagon from the blacksmith shop to the street, turned, and steered for the river. As they bumped up and down across the planks on the bridge, Billy Mac winced as the weight of the motion caused pain in his jaw and cheek. He put his hands to his face to bolster them.

Once across the bridge they turned south along the bluff on the dirt road that ran parallel to the river. A half hour later they could see the work zone. A little way farther they found a good spot to view the area they wanted. Joseph pulled the wagon off to the side of the road and set the hand brake.

Emmett turned from the bench seat, climbed into the wagon bed and stood up. He looked through his binoculars searching for the alcove until he found it. He hopped out of the wagon and walked a little farther along the bluff until he found a better vantage spot.

The other two boys jumped down from the wagon seat and followed. Billy Mac saw another wagon on the side of the road about a half-mile in front of them. It didn't look like there was anyone in it. Probably just other people who came to watch the blasting, too, he thought, and dismissed it.

"See anything, Emmo?" he asked.

"I can kind of see that open area where it curves around so the far wall faces us. Hard to see through some of the treetops that are sticking up over the bluff." He kept walking back and forth along the ridge with the binoculars help up to his eyes. He finally stopped and let the binocular fall to his chest, hanging on the strap around his neck. "There has to be a better way."

Emmett walked a little farther down the road, then turned and waved Billy Mac and Joseph on. "Hey! Check this out." He pointed at a ravine that ran down the bluff. He carefully walked down it a dozen feet until he was past the trees that had blocked his view from the road. Billy Mac and Joseph followed.

Emmett looked through the binoculars again. "Much better," he said, moving his head from side to side, scanning the area below them. "Wait—hold it. Oh, wow. Yeah. Hey, I can see that rock that we'd push out of the way but I can't see the opening to the cave. There's still some stuff sticking up farther down I can't see through. Oh, man! That bar of gold Ahote stole from the jailhouse—it's sitting on that rock! It's right there!"

"Yeah—I can see it from here," Billy Mac said. "You don't even need binoculars. I can see the sun reflecting off it."

Emmett let the binoculars hang down again and turned to Billy Mac and Joseph. "Guys," he started. "This ravine runs all the way down. It looks like it opens up pretty close to that alcove area. I'm going to get that gold. I can be down there and back in less than ten minutes."

"No way," Billy Mac objected. "We promised Pa we wouldn't do anything, not even get out of the wagon. And Doc. We promised Doc we'd take it easy for a few days, not even move around very much."

"I know, Mackie, but it's right there." Emmett pointed. "Just right there!"

"If you're going, we're coming with you," Joseph said.

Billy Mac hesitated, finally shrugged, and nodded. "Okay, but down and back. That's all. Nothing else. Deal?"

"Deal," the other two agreed.

Billy Mac walked around Emmett to lead the way. He got another dozen feet down the ravine, then stopped suddenly and held his arms out to keep the other two from going past him.

"What's wrong, Mackie?"

Billy Mac pointed. "Right there—right in front of us. The fox. Do you see it?"

"I don't see anything," Joseph answered.

"Me, neither," Emmett said.

"It's right there in the middle of the ravine, sitting, looking at us," Billy Mac said. "It's like before, Emmo—I'm the only who can see him."

"Can we walk around him, or just through him?" Emmett asked.

Billy Mac turned around and faced Emmett and Joseph. "We're not gonna do that. We're going to do what we should have done before. We're going to take his guidance. He's telling us there's danger down there. It's a warning. We're not going down there."

"It's only a few minutes, though, Mackie."

"Emmett, you're the smartest person I know. You drive me nuts sometimes you're so smart. You know more about everything than anyone I ever met. But right now, you're being stupid! We agreed, just last night, we'd pay attention to that fox spirit, my guardian spirit, if it ever showed itself again. We're not going down there and we're not letting you go down there. Right, Joseph?"

"Right," Joseph said and stepped forward to stand shoulder to shoulder with Billy Mac. They both puffed up and crossed their arms.

Emmett narrowed his eyes and looked at the two of them blocking his way down the ravine. Finally, he took a deep breath, slowly exhaled, nodded, and smiled that winsome way he always did. "You're right," he said. "We're not going down there."

The tension relieved, they all turned and looked back down into the alcove. Billy Mac noticed the fox was no longer there.

"Funny," Emmett said. "From down here you can see the whole thing. Now I can see the opening to that…wait! Do you see that? Someone's been digging in that cave! There's a pile of sand out in front of it!"

"You're right!" Billy Mac and Joseph both exclaimed.

A loud explosion shook the ground so much it felt like an earthquake; the boys had to catch their balance. Rocks and dirt broke away and tumbled down the ravine.

"Whoa!" Emmett said. "They're blasting—it's started!"

"Hey! Look!" Billy Mac pointed to the alcove. "Someone's crawling out of that cave!"

They watched as a person crawled his way out. While still on his hands and knees, he reached back into the cave and lifted something out with both hands. The person slowly stood up, walked over to the big rock, and put something on it next to the gold bar that was already there. Two somethings. And, they all looked the same, reflecting gold in the bright sun.

"Oh, my gosh!" Joseph said. "That's more gold! It's true! That's where it's all been hidden!"

"On, no," Billy Mac said slowly and shook his head. "Is that who I think it is?"

Emmett quickly put the binoculars back to his eyes. "It is. Jeez! What do we do?"

Another explosion sounded and shook the ground again. Billy Mac had to catch himself against the wall of the ravine to keep from falling. More rocks and dirt broke free and tumbled down around them.

In the alcove, Ahote stood still. After a few moments he flung himself back on the ground and quickly crawled into the cave.

"He's going back for more," Emmett cried. "We need to get back to town and find your pa, Mackie! C'mon!"

They all turned and started to scramble back up the ravine when two explosions went off at the same time. The double shock waves knocked the boys off their feet.

Then, a sharp, ear-piercing crack came from the cliffside above the alcove. The boys turned to watch as a massive section of the bluff broke free and crashed to the ground. Hundreds of tons of rock and dirt completely filled the alcove and poured into the grove in front of it, snapping trees from the tremendous force and weight of the avalanche.

The three boys stood in silence, trying to comprehend what they'd witnessed. Finally, a soft roar filled the air as they watched a wall of water flow through the trees, the start of backfill from the dam to form a new lake.

"That takes care of that," Emmett finally said. "Don't have to worry about him anymore."

"Or the gold," Billy Mac said quietly, still in awe of what he'd just seen.

"Or the gold," Joseph repeated. "Let's go," he said and started back up the ravine.

Emmett grabbed Billy Mac's shoulder to hold him in place. "Your guardian spirit saved us," he said to Billy Mac. "If it hadn't been for him, the three of us would be down there underneath all of that with Ahote" He pointed to what had been the alcove. "And, you and Joseph saved me. Thank you," he said and held out his hand.

"You bet," Billy Mac said and shook Emmett's hand.

"I envy you, Mackie," Emmett said.

"What?" Billy Mac exclaimed, surprised by Emmett's comment. "Why?"

"You have a new gift. I may know a lot of things because I read a lot, but you have a gift none of the rest of us will ever have. And, you have a guardian spirit that will help you all of your life. That's pretty neat." Emmett smiled.

Billy Mac was taken aback. He was the one who had always envied his friend, had always wished he could be more like him.

"Thanks, Emmett" was all he could think to say. The moment passed with a smile and the two of them turned to follow Joseph back up to the road.

"Emmo?" Billy Mac asked as they reached the top of the bluff. "Do you think you all can help me figure out more about that vision I can channel? Maybe what it all means, and maybe how I can use it?"

"Sure, Mackie," Emmett said and slapped him on the back. "We'll all figure it out, together."

They climbed onto the wagon and rode a half-mile farther down the road to the other wagon Billy Mac had noticed earlier. As they drew near, they recognized the horse as the one that had belonged to Ahote when he was posed as the character Taregan. The contents in the back of the wagon and the canvas cover folded up behind the bench seat confirmed it. Joseph turned his wagon around and headed back to the bridge. Emmett and Billy Mac followed in the other. Emmett was pretty good at driving a wagon.

Chapter 24

Emmett and Billy Mac stopped by the jailhouse, quickly briefed Billy Mac's father, and asked him to call Ms. Lee at the library and Principal Skinner. They'd been a part of the adventure from the beginning. The boys wanted to let them know how it had all concluded.

Then they drove the horse and wagon over to the livery. The representative from the Miami nation on his way to escort Taregan's body back home could take care of the horse and wagon, too.

They made their way back to the jailhouse just as Joseph arrived—he'd dropped his wagon at the blacksmith shop. They walked in to find everyone there, except Maddie. She waiting at the train station for her cousin to arrive from Indianapolis.

After small talk with Principal Skinner and Ms. Lee's inspection of Billy Mac's battered face, they all sat down. The boys brought them up to date, but purposely left out their short-lived decision to venture down to the alcove to retrieve the original bar of gold.

"Can't say I'm sorry to hear about Ahote," the sheriff shook his head. "He's been a pestilence to society most of his adult life."

"The incontestable loss of the hoard is most unfortunate, nevertheless," Principal Skinner said as he tapped his fingertips together. "Most unfortunate."

"Maybe someday," Miss Lee shrugged.

"Not for a while," the sheriff said. "There's no way the company that built that dam is going to jeopardize damage to it from some large-scale excavation so close to it."

Billy Mac jerked a thumb at Emmett. "Emmo here has decided he's gonna go to school to be a mechanical engineer. When he does, he'll be able to figure out something."

"Very admirable young man," Principal Skinner said to Emmett. "I'd be most pleased to converse with the dean at Purdue on your behalf. Their university would unquestionably profit from an intellect of your caliber."

Emmett glowed from the praise, a lopsided grin on his face.

"Well, I'll be," Billy Mac said. "First time I've ever seen him with nothing to say!"

The door opened; Maddie and her cousin walked in. Maddie was all smiles, carrying a small golden retriever puppy. Her head tilted to one side to keep her bangs out of her eyes.

"Looky here!" she cried. "Isn't he just adorable? My wonderful cousin brought him for me!" She hugged the puppy up to her face.

"Everyone," she continued, "this is my cousin Becky you've heard me talk so much about. She's a little shy so don't you embarrass her!" Maddie went on to introduce everyone one by one.

Billy Mac wasn't listening. Gosh, she was just as pretty as Maddie, he thought. A moment later their eyes met when Becky gave him a shy smile. He smiled back and Maddie caught him.

"He doesn't always look that handsome," Maddie said to Becky, poking fun at Billy Mac's face.

Billy Mac smiled at Maddie, walked over, and rubbed the puppy's head like used to do with Boomer. "Whatcha gonna name him, Maddie?"

"Well, when you put him down, he's pretty fast. How about 'Comet'?"

"Comet," Emmett repeated. "Yeah. That would be a great name."

Principal Skinner stood up. "Well, duty calls. Much to prepare prior to the academic year, which is nearly upon us. Very pleased to have you with us, my dear," he said to Becky. "Matilda, shall I walk you back to your library?"

"That would be nice," Ms. Lee answered. She turned to the boys and girls. "What in the world will you all do now? Find a new adventure?"

"None for me for a while," Billy Mac groaned.

"Well, visit me at the library to find a good read, or just to keep me up to date." She smiled and winked.

"First things first," Maddie said. "Mother is expecting us for a picnic at the farm."

"Want me to drive you all out?" the sheriff asked.

"It's so nice out," Maddie said. "Let's walk out on the tracks. We can show Becky the old cabin where this whole thing started and cross the creek. She's heard so much about it all."

"That would be nice," Becky agreed.

"Fine with me," Emmett said. "It's only about a mile or so. Okay with you, Mackie?"

"Sure," Billy Mac shrugged.

"Tell you what," Joseph said. "I've got a little more work to do at the shop. I'll drive out in the wagon after a while. That way, I can bring the guys back to town later."

A few minutes later Billy Mac, Emmett, Maddie—holding her puppy—and Becky were on the railroad tracks talking and walking toward the Miller farm.

Billy Mac, without thinking, did what came natural. He stepped onto one of the rails, held his arms out for balance, and walked without falling.

"Can I try?" Becky asked. It startled him and he slipped off.

"Well, sure," Billy Mac said. "It's easy."

"Easy for him," Emmett said. "I can't do it very well."

"You just have to know how," Billy Mac countered.

Becky stepped onto a rail, took a few steps, and slipped off. She stepped back up, took two more steps, and slipped off again.

Billy Mac stepped onto the rail and stood there. "Watch. Put your arms out for balance and stand still until you're ready. Then, don't look down at the rail; look straight ahead and just walk." He walked ten steps, then hopped down and came back to her. "Try it," he smiled at her.

"Will you help me?" She smiled and held her hand out.

Billy Mac froze, but only for a few seconds. He reached out, took her hand and the strangest feeling flipped in his stomach. He slowly helped her onto the rail. She stood there, smiled at him for a long moment, stretched out her other arm for balance, and slowly walked forward. Billy Mac walked with her and held her hand. He wasn't going to let go.

The End